D1711913

THE ULTIMATE
PHILADELPHIA PHILLIES
TRIVIA BOOK

A Collection of Amazing Trivia Quizzes
and Fun Facts for Die-Hard Phillies Fans!

Ray Walker

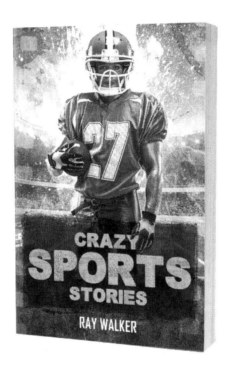

CONTENTS

INTRODUCTION

The Philadelphia Phillies were established in 1883. As one of the oldest teams in Major League Baseball, the Phillies have proven themselves to be a team that fights hard and is a force to be reckoned with in the MLB postseason.

They currently hold two World Series championships, which they won in 1980 and 2008. They have also won the National League Pennant seven times. They are very often a threat in the National League East Division, having won it 11 times total. Oddly enough, they do not yet have a wild card berth to their name.

The Phillies have retired the uniform numbers of Richie Ashburn, Jim Bunning, Mike Schmidt, Steve Carlton, and Robin Roberts. They also have a "Wall of Fame" at Citizens Bank Park to celebrate their past and the players and people who made it all possible.

The thing about baseball is that it is a lot like life. There are good times and bad times, good days and bad days, but you have to do your absolute best to never give up. The Philadelphia Phillies have proven that they refuse to give up and that they will do anything they need to do in order to bring a championship to the City of Brotherly Love.

Winning is more than possible when you have a storied past, as the Phillies do. They have so much captivating history and so many undeniable player legacies to be profoundly proud of.

The Phillies' current home is Citizens Bank Park, which opened in 2004. They play in one of the most difficult divisions in baseball, the National League East, along with the Atlanta Braves, Miami Marlins, New York Mets, and Washington Nationals.

With such a storied team past that goes back generations, you're probably already very knowledgeable as the die-hard Phillies fan that you are. Let's test that knowledge to see if you truly are the World's Biggest Phillies fan.

CHAPTER 1:

ORIGINS AND HISTORY

QUIZ TIME!

1. Which of the following team names did the Phillies franchise once go by?

    a. Quakers
    b. Blue Jays
    c. Eagles
    d. Both A and B

2. In what year was the Philadelphia Phillies franchise established?

    a. 1870
    b. 1883
    c. 1899
    d. 1901

3. The Phillies' current home stadium is Citizens Bank Park.

    a. True
    b. False

4. Which division do the Philadelphia Phillies play in?

    a. American League Central
    b. American League East
    c. National League East
    d. National League Central

5. The Philadelphia Phillies have never won a wild card berth.

    a. True
    b. False

6. How many National League Pennants has the Phillies franchise won (as of the 2020 season)?

    a. 3
    b. 7
    c. 9
    d. 12

7. What is the name of the Phillies' mascot?

    a. Phillie Filly
    b. Phillie Penguin
    c. Phillie Parrot
    d. Phillie Phanatic

8. Who is the longest-tenured manager in Philadelphia Phillies history (as of the 2020 season)?

    a. Larry Bowa
    b. Gene Mauch
    c. Charlie Manuel
    d. Eddie Sawyer

9. What is the name of the Philadelphia Phillies' Triple-A farm team and where is it located?

    a. Lehigh Valley IronPigs

    b. Scranton/Wilkes-Barre RailRiders

    c. Charlotte Knights

    d. Toledo Mud Hens

10. Who was the first manager of the franchise?

    a. Blondie Purcell

    b. Bob Ferguson

    c. Harry Wright

    d. Al Reach

11. The Phillies are the oldest continuous same-name, same-city franchise in American professional sports.

    a. True

    b. False

12. What is the name of the Phillies' current spring training home stadium?

    a. Ed Smith Stadium

    b. First Data Field

    c. Spectrum Field

    d. Hammond Stadium

13. How many appearances has the franchise made in the MLB playoffs (as of the 2020 season)?

    a. 9

    b. 11

    c. 14

    d. 18

14. How many World Series titles have the Phillies won (as of the 2020 season)?

   a. 1
   b. 2
   c. 3
   d. 4

15. The Phillies played in the American League East Division from 1969 through 1975.

   a. True
   b. False

16. What was the first home stadium of the Philadelphia Phillies' franchise?

   a. Connie Mack Stadium
   b. Veterans Stadium
   c. Recreation Park
   d. Baker Bowl

17. As of the 2020 season, how many National League Pennants have the Phillies won?

   a. 3
   b. 5
   c. 7
   d. 9

18. How many National League East Division titles have the Phillies won (as of the 2020 season)?

   a. 6
   b. 11

c. 15

d. 18

19. Which team is NOT currently in the National League East Division with the Phillies?

    a. Miami Marlins

    b. Washington Nationals

    c. New York Mets

    d. Chicago Cubs

20. Of all the teams in the NL East, the Phillies have won their division the most times.

    a. True

    b. False

QUIZ ANSWERS

1. D – Both A and B

2. B – 1883

3. A – True

4. C – National League East

5. A – True

6. B – 7

7. D – Phillie Phanatic

8. B – Gene Mauch

9. A – Lehigh Valley IronPigs

10. B – Bob Ferguson

11. A – True

12. C – Spectrum Field

13. C – 14

14. B – 2

15. B – False (They have always been in the National League East Division.)

16. C – Recreation Park

17. C – 7

18. B – 11

19. D – Chicago Cubs (they were a founding member of the NL East but moved to the NL Central in 1994).

20. B – False (Atlanta Braves)

DID YOU KNOW?

1. The Phillies have had 55 managers: Bob Ferguson, Blondie Purcell, Harry Wright, Jack Clements, Al Reach, Bob Allen, Arthur Irwin, Billy Nash, George Stallings, Bill Shettsline, Chief Zimmer, Hugh Duffy, Billy Murray, Red Dooin, Pat Moran, Jack Coombs, Gavvy Cravath, Bill Donovan, Kaiser Wilhelm, Art Fletcher, Stuffy McInnis, Burt Shotton, Jimmie Wilson, Hans Lobert, Bucky Harris, Freddie Fitzsimmons, Ben Chapman, Dusty Cooke, Eddie Sawyer, Steve O'Neill, Terry Moore, Mayo Smith, Andy Cohen, Gene Mauch, Bob Skinner, George Myatt, Frank Lucchesi, Paul Owens, Danny Ozark, Dallas Green, Pat Corrales, John Felske, Lee Elia, John Vukovich, Nick Leyva, Jim Fregosi, Terry Francona, Larry Bowa, Gary Varsho, Charlie Manuel, Ryne Sandberg, Pete Mackanin, Gabe Kapler, and Joe Girardi.

2. The Phillies' current manager is Joe Girardi. He previously managed the Florida Marlins in 2006 and the New York Yankees from 2008 to 2017. During his playing career as a catcher, he was with the Chicago Cubs, Colorado Rockies, New York Yankees, and the St. Louis Cardinals.

3. Charlie Manuel is the Philadelphia Phillies' all-time winningest manager with a record of 780-636 (.551) W-L%.

4. Robin Roberts was the first Phillie to have his number retired by the team. His number 36 was retired in 1962.

5. The Philadelphia Phillies have hosted three MLB All-Star Games so far. The first one took place in 1952 at Shibe Park, the second in 1976 at Veterans Stadium, and the third in 1996 at Veterans Park. The Phillies are slated to host the 2026 MLB All-Star Game at Citizens Bank Park.

6. Phillies pitchers have thrown 13 no-hitters. The first was thrown by Charles Ferguson in 1885 and the latest was thrown by Cole Hamels in 2015.

7. Two perfect games have been thrown in Phillies franchise history. The first was thrown by Jim Bunning in 1964 and the second was thrown by Roy Halladay in 2010.

8. The Phillies' Double-A farm team is the Reading Fightin' Phils. They have been the Double-A affiliate of the Phillies since 1967. They are currently tied for the longest affiliation in minor-league baseball.

9. The Phillies PA announcer is Dan Baker, who has held the job since the 1972 season.

10. The Phillie Phanatic is a large, furry, green flightless bird. He is originally from the Galápagos Islands and is the Phillies' biggest fan… or "phan."

CHAPTER 2:

JERSEYS AND NUMBERS

QUIZ TIME!

1. The current Phillies logo, team colors, and uniform date back to 1992.

   a. True
   b. False

2. The Phillies and which other team are the only MLB teams to have chain stitching on their chest emblems?

   a. New York Yankees
   b. Los Angeles Dodgers
   c. Toronto Blue Jays
   d. St. Louis Cardinals

3. In 2008, the Phillies introduced an alternate cream-colored uniform for home day games as a tribute to the franchise's 125th anniversary.

   a. True
   b. False

4. Which of the following numbers has NOT been retired by the Philadelphia Phillies (as of the end of the 2020 season)?

   a. 14
   b. 18
   c. 20
   d. 32

5. What uniform number does OF Bryce Harper wear as a member of the Phillies?

   a. 3
   b. 13
   c. 33
   d. 34

6. What uniform number did slugger Mike Schmidt wear during his time with the Phillies?

   a. 20
   b. 22
   c. 27
   d. Both A and B

7. The Phillies are the only team in the MLB who displays the player's number on one sleeve in addition to the usual placement on the back of the jersey.

   a. True
   b. False

8. Who is the only Phillies player to ever wear No. 0?

   a. Al Dark
   b. Rene Gonzales

c. Al Oliver

d. Mitch Williams

9. Which former Phillies legend had his No. 32 retired by the team?

a. Richie Ashburn

b. Jim Bunning

c. Robin Roberts

d. Steve Carlton

10. Throughout the 2009 season, the Phillies wore black circular "HK" patches over the hearts on their uniforms in memory of broadcaster Harry Kalas.

a. True

b. False

11. What are the Philadelphia Phillies' official team colors?

a. Burgundy, white, blue

b. Red, white, blue

c. Red, blue, burgundy

d. Red, white, blue, black

12. Who was the first Phillie to have his uniform number retired by the team?

a. Mike Schmidt

b. Chuck Klein

c. Richie Ashburn

d. Steve Carlton

13. RHP Robin Roberts is the latest to have his number (36) retired by the Phillies, on June 18, 2008.

a. True

b. False

14. What jersey number did Jim Bunning wear as a Phillie?

    a. 14

    b. 17

    c. 38

    d. Both A and C

15. What jersey number did Richie Ashburn wear as a Phillie?

    a. 1

    b. 11

    c. 21

    d. All of the Above

16. What jersey number did Chase Utley wear as a Phillie?

    a. 16

    b. 26

    c. 36

    d. Both A and B

17. What jersey number did Ryan Howard wear as a Phillie?

    a. 6

    b. 12

    c. 24

    d. Both A and B

18. What jersey number did Jimmy Rollins wear as a Phillie?

a. 6

b. 11

c. 29

d. All of the Above

19. What jersey number did Roy Halladay wear as a Phillie?

a. 32

b. 34

c. 52

d. None of the Above

20. Grover Cleveland Alexander and Chuck Klein are retired by the Phillies, but by letter, not number. The letter "P" represents them and their honor.

a. True

b. False

QUIZ ANSWERS

1. A – True

2. D – St. Louis Cardinals

3. A – True

4. B – 18

5. A – 3

6. D – Both A and B. Although No. 20 is retired by the Phillies, Schmidt did wear No. 22 in his rookie season.

7. A – True

8. C – Al Oliver

9. D – Steve Carlton

10. A – True

11. B – Red, white, blue

12. C – Richie Ashburn (Aug. 24, 1979)

13. A – True

14. A – 14

15. A – 1

16. B – 26

17. D – Both A and B

18. D – All of the Above

19. B – 34

20. A – True

DID YOU KNOW?

1. The Phillies are one of only four MLB teams who do not display their city, state, or region on their road jerseys. The other three teams who do not do this are the Los Angeles Angels of Anaheim, St. Louis Cardinals, and the Tampa Bay Rays.

2. In 2017, the Phillies revived their powder blue uniform as an alternate home uniform to be worn on select Thursday games.

3. During spring training, the Phillies wear solid red practice jerseys with red pinstripe pants at home and gray pants on the road. Back in 1977, the Phillies wore maroon V-neck uniforms during spring training.

4. In 1979, the Phillies debuted all-burgundy uniforms with white trimmings called the "Saturday Night Specials." They were only worn once due to outrage from fans. Many described the uniforms as "Pajama-like."

5. In 1994, the Phillies debuted all-blue hats on Opening Day. Players wanted them discontinued because they thought they were bad luck. A compromise was reached and they wore the blue hats for every weekday game and wore their red caps for Sunday games.

6. The Phillies have retired seven players and five numbers. Richie Ashburn's No. 1 was retired on Aug.

24, 1979, Jim Bunning's No. 14 on April 6, 2001, Mike Schmidt's No. 20 on May 26, 1990, Steve Carlton's No. 32 on July 29, 1989, Robin Robert's No. 36 on June 18, 2008. Grover Cleveland Alexander and Chuck Klein both had the letter "P" retired in their honor on April 6, 2001. Of course, Jackie Robinson's No. 42 is retired throughout MLB.

7. The Phillies do plan to retire the late Roy Halladay's No. 34. He will also have a statue in the Third Base Plaza of Citizens Bank Park. Halladay was posthumously named to the National Baseball Hall of Fame in 2019.

8. Three players have worn the No. 99 for the Phillies: Mitch Williams in 1993, Turk Wendell in 2001, and So Taguchi in 2008.

9. Pat Neshek is the only player ever to have worn No. 93 for the Phillies (at least so far). He wore it from 2018 to 2019.

10. Instead of a number on the back of his jersey, the Phillies' mascot, the Phillie Phanatic, has a star where his number would be.

CHAPTER 3:

FAMOUS QUOTES

QUIZ TIME!

1. Which former Phillie once said, "I never want to look in the mirror and say, 'What if? What if I had run harder? What if I had dived for that ground ball'"?

   a. Jimmy Rollins
   b. Mike Schmidt
   c. Steve Carlton
   d. Chase Utley

2. Which current Phillies player once said, "If you don't have dreams, you don't have a life. That's my motto"?

   a. Andrew McCutchen
   b. Bryce Harper
   c. Didi Gregorius
   d. Jake Arrieta

3. Which former Phillie is quoted as saying, "To cure a batting slump, I took my bat to bed with me. I wanted to know my bat a little better"?

a. Jayson Werth

b. Grover Cleveland Alexander

c. Richie Ashburn

d. Matt Stairs

4. Which former Phillie once said, "Underdog. That's something we've become accustomed to, playing in Philadelphia. We're always the underdog"?

a. Pete Rose

b. Jimmy Rollins

c. Tug McGraw

d. Shane Victorino

5. Which former Phillies pitcher is quoted as saying, "I've always tried to work hard. I'm not trying to show anybody up or do something spectacular for attention"?

a. Curt Schilling

b. Randy Wolf

c. Roy Halladay

d. Ryan Madson

6. Which former Phillie is quoted as saying, "I don't think I can get into my deep inner thoughts about hitting. It's like talking about religion"?

a. Mike Schmidt

b. Hunter Pence

c. Jim Thome

d. Pete Rose

7. Which former Phillies pitcher is Randy Johnson referring to?

8. "I had a long conversation with _____. He told me that on the days he pitched, he felt it was his responsibility to make everyone around him better, to lift his teammates. That's what I try to do." – Randy Johnson

   a. Jim Bunning
   b. Tug McGraw
   c. Jim Kaat
   d. Steve Carlton

9. Former Phillies OF Chuck Klein once said, "A life is not important except in the impact it has on other lives."

   a. True
   b. False

10. Which former Phillies manager is quoted as saying, "There's no pressure in baseball. Pressure is when the doctor is getting ready to cut you, take your heart out, and put it on a table"?

   a. Mayo Smith
   b. Charlie Manuel
   c. Dallas Green
   d. Jim Fregosi

11. Which former Phillies manager is quoted as saying, "You can't lead anyone else further than you have gone yourself"?

a. Gene Mauch

b. Terry Francona

c. Danny Ozark

d. Eddie Sawyer

12. Which Phillie is quoted as saying, "I'd walk through hell in a gasoline suit to play baseball"?

a. Mike Schmidt

b. Bryce Harper

c. Pete Rose

d. Joe Blanton

13. Which current MLB star is quoted as saying, "I grew up a Phillies fan. Me and my buddies tailgated a couple of times when they won the World Series. I like just being in that atmosphere"?

a. Aaron Judge

b. Anthony Rizzo

c. Nolan Arenado

d. Mike Trout

14. Which former Phillies player is quoted as saying, "I've talked to guys who have played for the Phillies and gone on to other organizations and the grass isn't always greener on the other side"?

a. John Kruk

b. Ryne Sandberg

c. Chase Utley

d. Ryan Howard

15. Which former Phillie is quoted as saying, "Rooting is following and I don't do that, but I'd like to see the Phillies win because I love Philadelphia"?

    a. Steve Carlton
    b. Lenny Dykstra
    c. Mike Schmidt
    d. Cole Hamels

16. Which former Phillies player is quoted as saying, "If I had to give advice about parents, it would be this: Value your relationships with them. Those relationships are what you stand for. Not only are we blessed to wear a uniform that says PHILLIES on the front, but we have our names on the back. That name means you're playing for your family"?

    a. Jamie Moyer
    b. Jim Thome
    c. Terry Mulholland
    d. Mitch Williams

17. Phillies pitcher Grover Alexander Cleveland once said, "Never allow the fear of striking out keep you from playing the game."

    a. True
    b. False

18. Which former Phillie is quoted as saying, "My father left me with a saying that I've carried my entire life and tried to pass on to our kids, 'Tough times don't last, tough people do'"?

a. John Kruk

b. Jim Bunning

c. Curt Schilling

d. Richie Ashburn

19. Which former Phillies player once said, "I can't stand satisfaction. To me, greatness comes from that quest for perfection"?

   a. Mike Schmidt

   b. Steve Carlton

   c. John Kruk

   d. Pete Rose

20. Which former Phillie once said, "You'd be surprised how many shortcomings can be overcome by hustle"?

   a. Mike Schmidt

   b. Pete Rose

   c. Steve Carlton

   d. Chase Utley

21. Former Phillie Scott Rolen once said, "I enjoy coming to the ballpark every day. I don't go to work. I come here to play."

   a. True

   b. False

QUIZ ANSWERS

1. D – Chase Utley

2. B – Bryce Harper

3. C – Richie Ashburn

4. B – Jimmy Rollins

5. C – Roy Halladay

6. A – Mike Schmidt

7. D – Steve Carson

8. B – False, Jackie Robinson

9. B – Charlie Manuel

10. A – Gene Mauch

11. C – Pete Rose

12. D – Mike Trout

13. C – Chase Utley

14. A – Steve Carlton

15. B – Jim Thome

16. B – False, Babe Ruth

17. C – Curt Schilling

18. A – Mike Schmidt

19. B – Pete Rose

20. A – True

DID YOU KNOW?

1. "Pete Rose is the most likable arrogant person I've ever met." – Mike Schmidt

2. "You feel like a rock star in some ways." – Cole Hamels on starting on Opening Day

3. "On some nights, you could totally predict that he was going to do something special." – A.J. Burnett on Roy Halladay

4. "I remember Reggie Jackson said: 'They don't boo nobodies.' I took that into consideration when I was 15, 16 years old." – Bryce Harper

5. "When Steve Carlton and I die, we're gonna be buried 60'6" apart." – Tim McCarver

6. "It's about focusing on the fight and not the fright." – Robin Roberts

7. "I avoided as much work as possible in the classroom but did all the work possible on the ballfield." – Chuck Klein

8. "I wish I'd known early what I had to learn late." – Richie Ashburn

9. "That's a clown question, bro." – Bryce Harper

10. "To both of the teams that we were blessed to be a part of — the Blue Jays and the Phillies. Thank you for

allowing us to grow up, to fail over and over, and finally learn how to succeed within your organizations. There were some really amazing years but there were some really tough ones, too, and you never gave up on him.

11. "More than anything, he would want both organizations to know that they hold a huge place in our heart and always will. Evidence of their love for us and our love for them, as well, was shown all week as they came together as one to celebrate Roy — and that means the world to me. To both organizations, I can't thank you enough.

12. "I think that Roy would want everyone to know that people are not perfect. We are all imperfect and flawed in one way or another. We all struggle, but with hard work, humility, and dedication, imperfect people can still have perfect moments. Roy was blessed in his life and in his career to have some perfect moments, but I believe that they were only possible because of the man he strived to be, the teammate that he was, and the people that he was so blessed to be on the field with." – Brandy Halladay's speech at the late Roy Halladay's National Baseball Hall of Fame Induction Ceremony

CHAPTER 4:

CATCHY NICKNAMES

QUIZ TIME!

1. Which nickname did P Steve Carlton go by?

   a. Stevey

   b. Carl

   c. Lefty

   d. Righty

2. Carlos Ruiz's nickname is "Chooch."

   a. True

   b. False

3. What was Roy Halladay's real first name?

   a. John

   b. Ryan

   c. Michael

   d. Harry

4. What was Roy Halladay's famous nickname?

   a. Hally

   b. Doc

c. Roy-Hall

d. Uncle

5. Which is NOT a nickname that has been applied to the Phillies as a team?

   a. The Phils

   b. The Fightin' Phils

   c. The Red Pinstripes

   d. The Lilies

6. Which nickname did Lenny Dykstra NOT go by?

   a. The Dude

   b. The Len Man

   c. Nails

   d. Dr. Dirt

7. Jimmy Rollins' nickname was "J-Roll."

   a. True

   b. False

8. Which nickname did Shane Victorino go by?

   a. Vic

   b. The Flyin' Hawaiian

   c. Super Shane

   d. Aloha

9. What nickname did former Phillie Richie Ashburn go by?

   a. Whitey

   b. Put-Put

c. Ashy

d. Both A and B

10. What is Mitch Williams' nickname?

    a. Willie

    b. Mitchie

    c. Wild Thing

    d. Crazy Mitch

11. What was Pete Rose's nickname?

    a. Rosie

    b. Prose

    c. Pete Hustle

    d. Charlie Hustle

12. Roy Halladay got the nickname "Doc" because he was a pediatrician during the baseball offseason.

    a. True

    b. False

13. What is Gary Matthew's nickname?

    a. Big G

    b. Sir

    c. Sarge

    d. Matty

14. What is Greg Luzinski's nickname?

    a. The Bull

    b. The Scorpion

    c. The Bulldog

    d. The Lion

15. Garry Maddox went by the nickname "The Secretary of Defense."

 a. True

 b. False

16. Which nickname was given to former Phillies closer Tug McGraw?

 a. TMG

 b. The Graw Man

 c. T-Graw

 d. Tugger

17. Former Phillies third baseman Willie Jones went by the nickname "Puddin' Head."

 a. True

 b. False

18. What nickname did former Phillies first baseman Dick Stuart go by?

 a. D-Stew

 b. Dr. Stewart

 c. Dr. Strangeglove

 d. Dr. Goldfinger

19. What was the nickname of former Phillies OF Bake McBride?

 a. The Baker Man

 b. Shake n Bake

 c. Bride n Groom

 d. Baker's Dozen

20. Chase Utley's nickname is "The Man."

    a. True
    b. False

QUIZ ANSWERS

1. C – Lefty

2. A – True

3. D – Harry

4. B – Doc

5. D – The Lilies

6. B – The Len Man

7. A – True

8. B – The Flyin' Hawaiian

9. D – Both A and B

10. C – Wild Thing

11. D – Charlie Hustle

12. B – False

13. C – Sarge

14. A – The Bull

15. A – True

16. D – Tugger

17. A – True

18. C – Dr. Strangeglove

19. B – Shake n Bake

20. A – True

DID YOU KNOW?

1. Former Phillie Pat Burrell was known as "Pat the Bat."

2. Former Phillie Mickey Morandini had the interesting nickname, "Dandy Little Glove Man."

3. Brad Lidge's nickname is "Lights Out."

4. Former Phillie Kevin Saucier was given the nickname "Hot Sauce" by fans.

5. Ryan Howard's nickname is "The Big Piece."

6. Former Phillie John Kruk goes by the nickname "Krukker."

7. Cole Hamels' nickname is "Hollywood."

8. Former Phillie Larry Bowa's nickname is "Gnat."

9. Mike Schmidt's nickname is simply "Schmitty."

10. Former Phillies catcher Darren Daulton's nickname is "Dutch."

CHAPTER 5:

SCHMITTY

QUIZ TIME!

1. What is Mike Schmidt's full name?

    a. Michael Gary Schmidt
    b. Michael James Schmidt
    c. Michael Edward Schmidt
    d. Michael Jack Schmidt

2. Mike Schmidt played his entire 18-season MLB career with the Philadelphia Phillies.

    a. True
    b. False

3. Where was Mike Schmidt born?

    a. Philadelphia, Pennsylvania
    b. San Diego, California
    c. Dayton, Ohio
    d. Portland, Oregon

4. When is Mike Schmidt's birthday?

    a. September 27, 1946
    b. September 27, 1949
    c. November 27, 1946
    d. November 27, 1949

5. Mike Schmidt was elected to the National Baseball Hall of Fame in 1995 with 96.5% of the vote.

    a. True
    b. False

6. On April 17, 1976, how many home runs did Mike Schmidt hit in one game?

    a. 3
    b. 4
    c. 5
    d. 6

7. How many MLB All-Star Games was Mike Schmidt named to during his career?

    a. 6
    b. 8
    c. 12
    d. 14

8. Mike Schmidt was a 3x National League MVP (1980, 1981, 1986).

    a. True
    b. False

9. Mike Schmidt was drafted by the Phillies in what round of the 1971 MLB draft?

   a. 1st
   b. 2nd
   c. 10th
   d. 15th

10. How many times did Mike Schmidt lead the National League in home runs?

    a. 5 times
    b. 8 times
    c. 10 times
    d. 12 times

11. How many times did Mike Schmidt lead the National League in RBI?

    a. 2 times
    b. 3 times
    c. 4 times
    d. 5 times

12. Mike Schmidt was named the 1980 World Series MVP.

    a. True
    b. False

13. How many Gold Glove Awards did Mike Schmidt win?

    a. 6
    b. 7
    c. 8
    d. 10

14. How many Silver Slugger Awards did Mike Schmidt win?

    a. 3
    b. 5
    c. 6
    d. 9

15. How many home runs did Mike Schmidt hit?

    a. 521
    b. 548
    c. 601
    d. 648

16. What is Mike Schmidt's career batting average?

    a. .250
    b. .259
    c. .267
    d. .299

17. Mike Schmidt stole 174 bases.

    a. True
    b. False

18. What year was Mike Schmidt's uniform number retired by the Phillies?

    a. 1990
    b. 1991
    c. 1992
    d. 1993

19. Where did Mike Schmidt attend college?

    a. University of Cincinnati
    b. Bowling Green State University
    c. Ohio State University
    d. Ohio University

20. Mike Schmidt made his MLB debut against the New York Mets and played his final MLB game against the Mets.

    a. True
    b. False

QUIZ ANSWERS

1. D – Michael Jack Schmidt

2. A – True

3. C – Dayton, Ohio

4. B – September 27, 1949

5. A – True

6. B – 4

7. C – 12

8. A – True

9. B – 2nd

10. B – 8 times (1974, 1975, 1976, 1980, 1981, 1983, 1984, 1986)

11. C – 4 times (1980, 1981, 1984, 1986)

12. A – True

13. D – 10

14. C – 6

15. B – 548

16. C – .267

17. A – True

18. A – 1990 (the year after he retired!)

19. D – Ohio University

20. B – False (he debuted against the Mets but his final game was against the San Francisco Giants.)

DID YOU KNOW?

1. In 2006, Mike Schmidt wrote a book called, Clearing the Bases: Juiced Players, Monster Salaries, Sham Records, and a Hall of Famer's Search for the Soul of Baseball.

2. Since 2002, Mike Schmidt has worked as a hitting coach with the Phillies during spring training.

3. In 2001, Mike Schmidt debuted a fishing tournament called, "Mike Schmidt Winner's Circle Invitational." The tournament helps raise money for cystic fibrosis.

4. In 2008, Mike Schmidt introduced a wine named Mike Schmidt 548 Zinfandel. The 548 is a reference to his career home runs stat. All proceeds went to cystic fibrosis.

5. Mike Schmidt battled Stage 3 melanoma but is now cancer-free. Wear sunscreen every day, people!

6. The most home runs Mike Schmidt hit in one season was in 1980 when he hit a whopping 48 home runs in 150 games played and 548 at-bats. He also had his highest RBI total for a season that year with 121. The Phils just so happened to win the World Series in 1980.

7. Mike Schmidt's batting average was an impressive .316 in 1981.

8. "Philadelphia is the only city where you can experience the thrill of victory and the agony of reading about it the next day." – Mike Schmidt

9. "There are things as a coach you can teach, but natural ability like the raw power [Schmidt] had is a rare gift you see maybe once in a lifetime." – Bob Wren, Mike Schmidt's coach at Ohio University

10. "If I had to do it all over again, I'd do it in Philadelphia. The only thing I'd change would be me. I would be less sensitive, more outgoing, and appreciative of what you expected from me." – Mike Schmidt in his National Baseball Hall of Fame induction speech

CHAPTER 6:

STATISTICALLY SPEAKING

QUIZ TIME!

1. Mike Schmidt holds the Philadelphia Phillies franchise record for the most home runs. How many did he hit?

    a. 382

    b. 450

    c. 548

    d. 568

2. Pitcher Steve Carlton has the most wins in Philadelphia Phillies franchise history with 241.

    a. True

    b. False

3. How many times have the Philadelphia Phillies appeared in the playoffs?

    a. 10

    b. 12

    c. 14

    d. 17

4. Which former Phillies batter holds the top FOUR single-season records for strikeouts with 199 in 2007 and 2008, 190 in 2014, and 186 in 2009?

    a. Mike Schmidt
    b. Jim Thome
    c. Marlon Byrd
    d. Ryan Howard

5. Which pitcher has the most strikeouts in Phillies franchise history with a whopping 3,031?

    a. Cole Hamels
    b. Steve Carlton
    c. Robin Roberts
    d. Curt Schilling

6. Who has the most stolen bases in Phillies franchise history with 510?

    a. Billy Hamilton
    b. Jimmy Rollins
    c. Ed Delahanty
    d. Sherry Magee

7. José Mesa holds the record for most saves in Phillies history with 123.

    a. True
    b. False

8. Who is the Phillies' all-time winningest manager?

    a. Kaiser Wilhelm
    b. Eddie Sawyer

c. Charlie Manuel

d. Danny Ozark

9. Which player holds the Phillies franchise record for home runs in a single season with 58?

a. Ryan Howard

b. Mike Schmidt

c. Jim Thome

d. Cy Williams

10. Who holds the single-season Phillies record with 254 hits?

a. Richie Ashburn

b. Sam Thompson

c. Chuck Klein

d. Lefty O'Doul

11. Which two players are tied for the single-season Phillies record for double plays grounded into with 25 each?

a. Del Ennis and David Bell

b. Del Ennis and Ted Sizemore

c. Glenn Wilson and Ted Sizemore

d. David Bell and Ted Sizemore

12. Chase Utley holds the record for the most sacrifice flies in Phillies history with 108.

a. True

b. False

13. Steve Carlton threw how many of the wildest pitches in Phillies franchise history?

a. 64

b. 71

c. 120

d. 145

14. Sam Thompson holds the Phillies single-season record for most triples. How many did he hit in his record 1894 season?

    a. 28

    b. 23

    c. 21

    d. 20

15. Which hitter has the most walks in Phillies franchise history with 1,507?

    a. Bobby Abreu

    b. Jimmy Rollins

    c. Chase Utley

    d. Mike Schmidt

16. Which Phillies hitter holds the all-time franchise record for best overall batting average at .360?

    a. Nap Lajoie

    b. Billy Hamilton

    c. Elmer Flick

    d. Spud Davis

17. Mike Schmidt has the most games played as a Phillie and holds the Phillies record for WAR, plate appearances, runs scored, total bases, home runs, RBI, walks, extra-

base hits, sacrifice flies, intentional walks, and times on base.

    a. True

    b. False

18. Mike Schmidt has the most plate appearances of all time in Phillies franchise history. How many did he have?

    a. 9,511

    b. 9,876

    c. 10,062

    d. 10,099

19. Which pitcher holds the Phillies franchise record for most saves in a single season with 45?

    a. Mitch Williams

    b. Jonathan Papelbon

    c. Brad Lidge

    d. José Mesa

20. Robin Roberts holds the Phillies franchise record for most losses with 199.

    a. True

    b. False

QUIZ ANSWERS

1. C – 548

2. A – True

3. C – 14

4. D – Ryan Howard

5. B – Steve Carlton

6. A – Billy Hamilton

7. B – False, Jonathan Papelbon

8. C – Charlie Manuel (780-636, .551 W-L%)

9. A – Ryan Howard (2006)

10. D – Lefty O'Doul (1929)

11. B – Del Ennis (1950) and Ted Sizemore (1977)

12. B – False, Mike Schmidt

13. C – 120

14. A – 28

15. D – Mike Schmidt

16. B – Billy Hamilton

17. A – True

18. C – 10, 062

19. D – José Mesa (2002)

20. A – True

DID YOU KNOW?

1. Robin Roberts threw the most innings in Phillies franchise history with 3,739.1. Coming in second is Steve Carlton with 3,697.1 innings.

2. Tuck Turner had the best single-season batting average in Phillies franchise history at .418 in 1894. Sam Thompson comes in the second spot with a batting average of .415 the same season.

3. Chase Utley holds the Phillies franchise record for stolen base percentage with 88.57% success. Billy Hamilton holds the Phillies franchise record for stolen bases with 510. Richie Ashburn holds the Phillies franchise record for the most times caught stealing with 100.

4. Mike Schmidt has the most extra-base hits in Phillies franchise history with 1,015. Second on the list is Jimmy Rollins with 806.

5. Jim Thome holds the Phillies franchise record for at-bats per home run with 13.3. This means that during his time with Philadelphia, Thome hit a home run about every 13-14 at-bats.

6. Aaron Nola holds the Phillies franchise record for strikeouts per 9 innings pitched with 9.743, meaning that he recorded about 9-10 strikeouts in every 9 innings that he pitched for the team.

7. Pitcher Tom Vickery holds the single-season Phillies record for the most hit by pitches with 29 in 1890.

8. Del Ennis and Granny Hamner are tied for the Phillies franchise record for double plays grounded into with 171 each.

9. Kid Gleason holds the Phillies single-season record for wins with 38 in 1890. Second on the list is Pete Alexander with 33 in 1916.

10. John Coleman holds the Phillies record for the most losses pitched in a single season with 48 in 1883. Charlie Ferguson is second on the list with 25 in 1884.

CHAPTER 7:

THE TRADE MARKET

QUIZ TIME!

1. On February 25, 1972, the Philadelphia Phillies traded RHP Rick Wise to the St. Louis Cardinals for which player?

    a. Woodie Fryman

    b. Ken Reynolds

    c. Steve Carlton

    d. Jim Nash

2. On December 16, 2009, the Phillies traded C Travis d'Arnaud, RHP Kyle Drabek, and OF Michael Taylor to the St. Louis Cardinals in exchange for cash and which player?

    a. Jamie Moyer

    b. Roy Halladay

    c. J.A. Happ

    d. Roy Oswalt

3. The Philadelphia Phillies have NEVER made a trade with the Colorado Rockies.

   a. True
   b. False

4. On April 2, 1992, the Philadelphia Phillies traded RHP Jason Grimsley to the Houston Astros in exchange for which player?

   a. Curt Schilling
   b. Terry Mulholland
   c. Greg Mathews
   d. Mitch Williams

5. The Philadelphia Phillies have made only six trades with the Arizona Diamondbacks all time (as of the end of the 2019 season).

   a. True
   b. False

6. In what year did the Philadelphia Phillies acquire RHP Jim Bunning and C Gus Triandos from the Detroit Tigers?

   a. 1960
   b. 1961
   c. 1963
   d. 1965

7. On November 18, 1997, the Philadelphia Phillies traded SS Kevin Stocker to the Tampa Bay Devil Rays in exchange for which player?

a. Mark Lewis

b. Doug Glanville

c. Scott Rolen

d. Bobby Abreu

8. Which team traded LHP Cliff Lee to the Philadelphia Phillies on July 29, 2009?

a. Cleveland Indians

b. Texas Rangers

c. New York Mets

d. Seattle Mariners

9. On July 17, 2008, the Philadelphia Phillies traded Josh Outman, Adrian Cardenas, and Matthew Spencer to the Oakland A's in exchange for which player?

a. Adam Eaton

b. Jimmy Rollins

c. Matt Stairs

d. Joe Blanton

10. The Philadelphia Phillies have only made six trades with the Miami Marlins (as of the end of the 2019 season).

a. True

b. False

11. On July 29, 2010, the Philadelphia Phillies traded Anthony Gose, J.A. Happ, and Jonathan Villar to the Houston Astros in exchange for _____.

a. J.C. Romero

b. Raul Ibañez

    c. Roy Oswalt

    d. Placido Polanco

12. The Philadelphia Phillies have made only six trades with the Kansas City Royals (as of the end of the 2019 season).

    a. True

    b. False

13. How many trades have the Philadelphia Phillies made with the San Diego Padres all time (as of the 2019 season)?

    a. 5

    b. 10

    c. 15

    d. 20

14. The Philadelphia Phillies NEVER traded Ryan Howard.

    a. True

    b. False

15. At the trade deadline in 2015, the Philadelphia Phillies traded Cole Hamels and Jake Diekman, along with cash, to which team in exchange for Jorge Alfaro, Alec Asher, Jerad Eickhoff, Matt Harrison, Jake Thompson, and Nick Williams?

    a. Chicago Cubs

    b. Toronto Blue Jays

    c. Los Angeles Dodgers

    d. Texas Rangers

16. On July 29, 2002, the Philadelphia Phillies traded Doug Nickle, this player, and cash to the St. Louis Cardinals in exchange for Mike Timlin, Bud Smith, and which player?

    a. Scott Rolen, J.D. Drew
    b. Doug Glanville, J.D. Drew
    c. Scott Rolen, Placido Polanco
    d. Doug Glanville, Placido Polanco

17. How many trades have the Philadelphia Phillies made with the Los Angeles Dodgers (as of the 2019 season)?

    a. 5
    b. 10
    c. 15
    d. 20

18. On July 26, 2000, the Philadelphia Phillies traded Curt Schilling to which team in exchange for Omar Daal, Nelson Figueroa, Travis Lee, and Vicente Padilla?

    a. Arizona Diamondbacks
    b. Boston Red Sox
    c. Baltimore Orioles
    d. Houston Astros

19. On December 6, 2006, the Philadelphia Phillies traded Gio Gonzalez and Gavin Floyd to which team in exchange for Freddy Garcia?

    a. Oakland Athletics
    b. Washington Nationals

c. Chicago White Sox

d. Milwaukee Brewers

20. In 1966, the Phillies traded Fergie Jenkins to the Chicago Cubs.

a. True

b. False

QUIZ ANSWERS

1. C – Steve Carlton

2. B – Roy Halladay

3. B – False (four trades as of the end of the 2019 season)

4. A – Curt Schilling

5. A – True

6. C – 1963

7. D – Bobby Abreu

8. A – Cleveland Indians

9. D – Joe Blanton

10. A – True

11. C – Roy Oswalt

12. A – True

13. C – 15

14. A – True

15. D – Texas Rangers

16. C – Scott Rolen, Placido Polanco

17. D – 20

18. A – Arizona Diamondbacks

19. C – Chicago White Sox

20. A – True

DID YOU KNOW?

1. On November 7, 2007, the Philadelphia Phillies traded OF Michael Bourn, RHP Geoff Geary, and INF Mike Costanzo to the Houston Astros in exchange for RHP Brad Lidge and INF Eric Bruntlett.

2. On June 18, 1989, the Philadelphia Phillies traded INF/OF Juan Samuel to the New York Mets in exchange for OF Lenny Dykstra, RHP Roger McDowell, and Tom Edens.

3. On February 23, 1979, the Philadelphia Phillies traded INF Ted Sizemore, OF Jerry Martin, C Barry Foote, RHP Derek Botelho, and RHP Henry Mack to the Chicago Cubs in exchange for 2B Manny Trillo, OF Greg Gross, and C Dave Rader.

4. On December 26, 1917, the Philadelphia Phillies traded OF Dode Paskert to the Chicago Cubs in exchange for OF Cy Williams. Cy Williams supposedly did not get along with the Cubs manager, Fred Mitchell.

5. Curt Flood viewed Philadelphia as a racist city and refused to accept a trade to the Phillies from the St. Louis Cardinals in 1969.

6. In 1958, the Philadelphia Phillies traded P Jack Sanford to the San Francisco Giants in exchange for C Valmy Thomas and P Ruben Gomez.

7. In 1983, the Philadelphia Phillies traded P Willie Hernandez and 1B Dave Bergman to the Detroit Tigers in exchange for C John Wockenfuss and OF Glenn Wilson.

8. In 1917, the Philadelphia Phillies traded P Grover Cleveland Alexander and C Bill Kiefer to the Chicago Cubs in exchange for P Mike Prendergast, C Pickles Dillhoefer, and $60,000. Owner William Baker needed money and feared he would lose Alexander to the WWI draft anyway.

9. In 1982, the Philadelphia Phillies traded 2B Ryne Sandberg and SS Larry Bowa to the Chicago Cubs in exchange for SS Ivan DeJesus.

10. In February of 2019, the Philadelphia Phillies signed free agent OF Bryce Harper to a 13-year, $330 million contract. He is among the highest-paid baseball players of all time.

CHAPTER 8:

DRAFT DAY

QUIZ TIME!

1. Which MLB team drafted former Phillie Jim Thome in the 13th round of the 1989 MLB draft?

    a. Baltimore Orioles

    b. Chicago White Sox

    c. Minnesota Twins

    d. Cleveland Indians

2. With the 17th overall pick in the first round of the 2002 MLB draft, the Philadelphia Phillies selected which player?

    a. Cory Lidle

    b. Cole Hamels

    c. Ryan Madson

    d. Kyle Lohse

3. The Philadelphia Phillies selected 1B Ryan Howard in the 5th round of the 2001 MLB draft from which college?

    a. San Diego State University

    b. University of Missouri

c. Missouri State University

d. Sacramento State University

4. With which overall pick in the first round of the 1995 MLB draft did the Toronto Blue Jays select RHP Roy Halladay?

a. 1st

b. 7th

c. 10th

d. 17th

5. With the 2nd overall pick in the first round of the 1997 MLB draft, the Philadelphia Phillies selected OF J.D. Drew from which school?

a. Florida State University

b. University of Florida

c. Oregon State University

d. University of Oregon

6. With the 15th overall pick in the first round of the 2000 MLB draft, the Philadelphia Phillies selected which player out of UCLA?

a. Chase Utley

b. Ryan Howard

c. Bobby Abreu

d. Doug Glanville

7. The Philadelphia Phillies drafted Bryce Harper with the first overall pick in the 2010 MLB draft.

a. True

b. False

8. LHP Jamie Moyer was drafted in the 6th round of the 1984 MLB draft by which team?

   a. Baltimore Orioles
   b. Seattle Mariners
   c. Texas Rangers
   d. Chicago Cubs

9. Mike Schmidt was drafted by the Philadelphia Phillies in what round of the 1971 MLB draft?

   a. 1st
   b. 2nd
   c. 5th
   d. 8th

10. Marlon Byrd was drafted by the Philadelphia Phillies in the 10th round of the 1999 MLB draft.

   a. True
   b. False

11. In the first round of the 2005 MLB draft, the Pittsburgh Pirates selected current Phillies outfielder Andrew McCutchen at which place overall?

   a. 1st
   b. 4th
   c. 7th
   d. 11th

12. John Mabry was drafted by the Philadelphia Phillies in the 6th round of the 1991 MLB draft.

   a. True
   b. False

13. With the first overall pick in the first round of the 1998 MLB draft, the Philadelphia Phillies chose which player out of the University of Miami?

    a. Travis Lee
    b. Doug Glanville
    c. Pat Burrell
    d. Scott Rolen

14. The Philadelphia Phillies selected SS Jimmy Rollins in the 2nd round of the MLB draft in which year?

    a. 1994
    b. 1995
    c. 1996
    d. 1998

15. RHP A.J. Burnett was drafted by which team in the 8th round of the 1995 MLB draft?

    a. Florida Marlins
    b. New York Yankees
    c. Pittsburgh Pirates
    d. New York Mets

16. Third baseman Scott Rolen was drafted in the 2nd round of the 1993 MLB draft by which team?

    a. Philadelphia Phillies
    b. St. Louis Cardinals
    c. Cincinnati Reds
    d. Toronto Blue Jays

17. With the 37th overall pick in the first round of the 2007 MLB draft, the Philadelphia Phillies selected which player?

    a. Carlos Ruiz

    b. Travis d'Arnaud

    c. John Mayberry

    d. Placido Polanco

18. RHP Ryan Madson was drafted by the Philadelphia Phillies in which round of the 1998 MLB draft?

    a. 3rd

    b. 7th

    c. 9th

    d. 12th

19. RHP Joe Blanton was drafted in the first round, 24th overall in the 2002 MLB draft by which team?

    a. Los Angeles Dodgers

    b. Kansas City Royals

    c. Pittsburgh Pirates

    d. Oakland A's

20. With the 3rd overall pick in the 1974 MLB draft, the Philadelphia Phillies chose OF Lonnie Smith.

    a. True

    b. False

QUIZ ANSWERS

1. D – Cleveland Indians

2. B – Cole Hamels

3. C – Missouri State University

4. D – 17th

5. A – Florida State University

6. A – Chase Utley

7. B – False, Washington Nationals

8. D – Chicago Cubs

9. B – 2nd

10. A – True

11. D – 11th

12. B – False, St. Louis Cardinals

13. C – Pat Burrell

14. C – 1996

15. D – New York Mets

16. A – Philadelphia Phillies

17. B – Travis d' Arnaud

18. C – 9th

19. D – Oakland A's

20. A – True

DID YOU KNOW?

1. The New York Mets selected former Phillies CF Lenny Dykstra in the 13th round of the 1981 MLB draft.

2. The Chicago Cubs drafted former Phillies CF Doug Glanville in the 1st round, 12th overall, in the 1991 MLB draft.

3. The Boston Red Sox drafted former Phillies RHP Curt Schilling in the 2nd round of the 1986 MLB draft.

4. The St. Louis Cardinals drafted former Phillies INF Placido Polanco in the 19th round of the 1994 MLB draft.

5. The Los Angeles Dodgers drafted former Phillies OF Shane Victorino in the 6th round of the 1999 MLB draft.

6. The Baltimore Orioles drafted former Phillies OF Jayson Werth in the first round, 22nd overall in the 1997 MLB draft.

7. The Minnesota Twins drafted former Phillies LHP J.C. Romero in the 21st round of the 1997 MLB draft.

8. The Philadelphia Phillies drafted LHP J.A. Happ in the 3rd round of the 2004 MLB draft out of Northwestern University.

9. The Montreal Expos drafted former Phillies LHP Cliff Lee in the 4th round of the 2000 MLB draft.

10. The Baltimore Orioles drafted current Phillies RHP Jake Arrieta in the 5th round of the 2007 MLB draft.

CHAPTER 9:

ODDS AND ENDS

QUIZ TIME!

1. Ryan Howard appeared on which TV sitcom that featured a character with the same name?

    a. Parks and Recreation

    b. The Office

    c. Brooklyn Nine Nine

    d. New Girl

2. Ryan Howard also appeared in an episode of *Entourage* in which he played himself.

    a. True

    b. False

3. Bryce Harper is a fan of which NHL team?

    a. San Jose Sharks

    b. Philadelphia Flyers

    c. Washington Capitals

    d. Vegas Golden Knights

4. Cole Hamels' wife Heidi was a contestant on which TV reality show?

    a. Big Brother
    b. American Ninja Warrior
    c. Survivor
    d. The Amazing Race

5. Shane Victorino was on an episode of which TV show, playing a character named Shaun?

    a. Hawaii Five-0
    b. CSI
    c. Law and Order SVU
    d. NCIS

6. Andrew McCutchen proposed to his longtime girlfriend, Maria on which talk show?

    a. The Tonight Show with Jimmy Fallon
    b. The Late Late Show with James Corden
    c. The View
    d. The Ellen DeGeneres Show

7. Chase Utley and Ryan Howard appeared on an episode of *It's Always Sunny in Philadelphia*, playing themselves in 2010.

    a. True
    b. False

8. Jamie Moyer and his ex-wife, Karen were introduced by which famous baseball broadcaster?

    a. Vin Scully
    b. Bob Uecker

c. Harry Caray

d. Tim McCarver

9. Hunter Pence proposed to his girlfriend Alexis at which famous theme park?

   a. Disneyland

   b. Walt Disney World

   c. Universal Studios Hollywood

   d. Knott's Berry Farm

10. Pat Burrell had an English bulldog who was featured in the Phillies' 2008 World Series parade and was named what?

   a. Prince

   b. Sinatra

   c. Elvis

   d. Bowie

11. Which famous MLB player is the godfather of Placido Polanco's son Ishmael?

   a. Albert Pujols

   b. Robinson Cano

   c. José Altuve

   d. Manny Machado

12. Country singer Tim McGraw is the son of former Phillies pitcher Tug McGraw.

   a. True

   b. False

13. Lenny Dykstra's son, Cutter is in a relationship with which actress?

    a. Dakota Johnson
    b. Lea Michele
    c. Anna Kendrick
    d. Jamie Lynn Sigler

14. Which former Phillie is now an analyst for MLB Network?

    a. Jim Kaat
    b. Pedro Martinez
    c. Mike Schmidt
    d. Both A and B

15. Jake Arrieta was a groomsman in which MLB player's wedding?

    a. Kris Bryant
    b. Matt Carpenter
    c. Anthony Rizzo
    d. Adam Wainwright

16. Dale Sveum is the cousin of former Toronto Blue Jays player John Olerud.

    a. True
    b. False

17. Kyle Kendrick's wife Stephanie was a three-time contestant on which TV reality show?

    a. Big Brother
    b. American Ninja Warrior

c. Survivor

d. The Amazing Race

18. When he was a kid growing up in Las Vegas, Bryce Harper played baseball with which current MLB star?

   a. Kris Bryant

   b. Joey Gallo

   c. Mike Trout

   d. Both A and B

19. Early in his career, A.J. Burnett named his bats after songs by which musical artist(s)?

   a. Panic! at the Disco

   b. Marilyn Manson

   c. Madonna

   d. Michael Jackson

20. A species of weevil, *Sicoderus bautistai,* was named after José Bautista in 2018.

   a. True

   b. False

QUIZ ANSWERS

1. B – The Office

2. A – True

3. D – Vegas Golden Knights

4. C – Survivor

5. A – Hawaii Five-0

6. D – The Ellen DeGeneres Show

7. A – True

8. C – Harry Caray

9. B – Walt Disney World

10. C – Elvis

11. A – Albert Pujols

12. A – True

13. D – Jamie Lynn Sigler

14. D – Both A and B

15. B – Matt Carpenter

16. A – True

17. C – Survivor

18. D – Both A and B

19. B – Marilyn Manson

20. A – True

DID YOU KNOW?

1. Curt Schilling is one of only 11 players born in the state of Alaska to play in the MLB.

2. Shane Victorino and his family were on an episode of the show, *Tanked*. Brett Raymer and Wayde King made the family a baseball cap fish tank and installed it next to the staircase in their home.

3. Jim Thome established a fund during his playing days to help put his 10 nieces and nephews through college.

4. Hunter Pence appeared in an episode of *Fuller House*, playing himself. He also appeared on an episode of *Bill Nye Saves the World*.

5. In 2012, Jake Arrieta appeared on an episode of the HBO show, *Veep*. In 2017, he appeared in an episode of *Chicago Fire* alongside former teammate Kris Bryant.

6. During the 2008 season, as a member of the Detroit Tigers, Placido Polanco became a naturalized American citizen. He took his oath of citizenship during a pregame ceremony at Comerica Park.

7. Bryce Harper is known for hitting home runs on Opening Day. He became the first player in MLB history to hit five home runs in Opening Day games before the age of 25.

8. Roy Halladay was the first player to be inducted into the

National Baseball Hall of Fame posthumously since Roberto Clemente in 1973.

9. Bryce Harper has a dog named "Wrigley." The man clearly loves baseball.

10. Charlie Manuel has survived a heart attack, quadruple bypass surgery, kidney cancer, and a blocked, infected colon.

CHAPTER 10:

OUTFIELDERS

QUIZ TIME!

1. Raul Ibañez played the seasons with the Philadelphia Phillies. Which of the following teams did he NOT play for during his 19-season career?

    a. Seattle Mariners

    b. New York Yankees

    c. Minnesota Twins

    d. Kansas City Royals

2. Former Phillies left fielder Pat Burrell was never named to an MLB All-Star Game in his 12-year MLB career.

    a. True

    b. False

3. How many Gold Glove Awards did former Phillie Pete Rose win during his 24-year MLB career?

    a. 0

    b. 2

    c. 5

    d. 10

4. Marlon Byrd was named to only one MLB All-Star Game in his 15-year MLB career.

   a. True
   b. False

5. Jayson Werth played four seasons with the Philadelphia Phillies. Which of the following teams did he NOT play for during his 15-season career?

   a. Washington Nationals
   b. Texas Rangers
   c. Los Angeles Dodgers
   d. Toronto Blue Jays

6. Former Phillies left fielder Greg Luzinski played for two teams in his 15-season MLB career; the Phillies and which team?

   a. Cleveland Indians
   b. Arizona Diamondbacks
   c. Boston Red Sox
   d. Chicago White Sox

7. Shane Victorino played his entire 12-year MLB career with the Phillies.

   a. True
   b. False

8. How many seasons did outfielder Hunter Pence play for the Phillies?

   a. 1
   b. 2

c. 3

d. 4

9. How many home runs did Jayson Werth hit for the Phillies during the 2009 season?

a. 24

b. 27

c. 36

d. 44

10. How many seasons did outfielder Pat Burrell play for the Philadelphia Phillies?

a. 2

b. 5

c. 7

d. 9

11. John Kruk played for six seasons with the Philadelphia Phillies. He also played for the Chicago White Sox and which other team?

a. San Diego Padres

b. Los Angeles Dodgers

c. Boston Red Sox

d. Atlanta Braves

12. Marlon Byrd was named NL Rookie of the Year in 2003.

a. True

b. False

13. How many home runs did former Phillies outfielder Juan Pierre hit during his one season in Philadelphia?

a. 0

b. 1

c. 3

d. 5

14. How many games did John Mayberry play for the Phillies during his five seasons in Philadelphia?

    a. 300

    b. 400

    c. 500

    d. 600

15. How many bases did Pete Rose steal during his five years as a Phillie?

    a. 45

    b. 51

    c. 55

    d. 61

16. How many games did Jeff Francoeur play for the Phillies during the 2015 season?

    a. 99

    b. 101

    c. 110

    d. 118

17. How many times was former Phillie Pete Rose named to the MLB All-Star Game?

    a. 9 times

    b. 14 times

c. 17 times

d. 20 times

18. How many triples did Shane Victorino hit for the Phillies during the 2011 season?

    a. 16

    b. 15

    c. 14

    d. 13

19. How many seasons did Chuck Klein spend with the Philadelphia Phillies?

    a. 3 years

    b. 10 years

    c. 15 years

    d. 17 years

20. Lonnie Smith played for two MLB teams in his 17-season career; the Phillies and the Atlanta Braves.

    a. True

    b. False

QUIZ ANSWERS

1. C – Minnesota Twins

2. A – True

3. B – 2

4. A – True

5. B – Texas Rangers

6. D – Chicago White Sox

7. B – False [Boston Red Sox (3 years), Los Angeles Dodgers (1 year), San Diego Padres (1 year), Los Angeles Angels of Anaheim (1 year)]

8. B – 2

9. C – 36

10. D – 9

11. A – San Diego Padres

12. B – False (He finished in 4th place; Dontrelle Willis was named the NL Rookie of the Year.)

13. B – 1

14. C – 500

15. B – 51

16. D – 118

17. C – 17 times

18. A – 16

19. C – 15 years

20. B – False [Six teams: Atlanta Braves (5 years), Phillies (4 years), St. Louis Cardinals (4 years), Kansas City Royals (3 years), Baltimore Orioles (2 years), Pittsburgh Pirates (1 year)]

DID YOU KNOW?

1. Bryce Harper hit 35 home runs in his first season as a Phillie. He played in 157 games and collected 114 RBIs.

2. Pat Burrell played 1,306 games for the Philadelphia Phillies, the most of any team he played for during his 12-year MLB career. He also played for the Tampa Bay Rays and the San Francisco Giants.

3. Marlon Byrd played 410 games for the Phillies, the most of any team he played for during his 15-year MLB career. He also played for the Texas Rangers, Chicago Cubs, Washington Nationals, New York Mets, San Francisco Giants, Pittsburgh Pirates, Boston Red Sox, Cleveland Indians, and the Cincinnati Reds.

4. Greg Luzinski played 1,289 games total for the Philadelphia Phillies, the most of any team he played for during his 15-year MLB career. He also played for the Chicago White Sox.

5. Lenny Dykstra played 734 games total for the Philadelphia Phillies, the most of any team he played for during his 12-year MLB career. He also played for the New York Mets.

6. In his 24-season MLB career, Pete Rose was named MVP, Rookie of the Year, was a 17x All-Star, 3x World Series Champion, 2x Gold Glove Award winner, Silver

Slugger Award winner, World Series MVP, and he won three batting titles.

7. Lonnie Smith was a 1x All-Star and 3x World Series Champion. He played In 196 games during his four years in Philadelphia.

8. Jeff Francoeur played 118 games total for the Philadelphia Phillies. During his 12-season career, he also played for the Atlanta Braves, Kansas City Royals, New York Mets, San Francisco Giants, Texas Rangers, San Diego Padres, and the Miami Marlins.

9. Andrew McCutchen hit 10 home runs in his first season in Philly. He has also played for the Pittsburgh Pirates, New York Yankees, and the San Francisco Giants.

10. Bryce Harper was named the 2012 National League Rookie of the Year as a member of the Washington Nationals. He was also named to his first MLB All-Star Game that year.

CHAPTER 11:

INFIELDERS

QUIZ TIME!

1. Chase Utley played for two MLB teams during his 16-season career: the Phillies and which other team?

    a. Seattle Mariners
    b. Minnesota Twins
    c. San Diego Padres
    d. Los Angeles Dodgers

2. Mike Schmidt played his entire 18-season MLB career with the Phillies.

    a. True
    b. False

3. How many stolen bases did former Phillies shortstop Jimmy Rollins record during his 2001 season?

    a. 29
    b. 37
    c. 46
    d. 55

4. How many home runs did former Phillies first baseman Ryan Howard hit during his 2006 season?

    a. 45
    b. 48
    c. 58
    d. 60

5. Former Phillies shortstop Larry Bowa was the Phillies' manager from 2001 to 2004. What team did he manage from 1987 to 1988?

    a. Chicago Cubs
    b. San Diego Padres
    c. New York Mets
    d. Cincinnati Reds

6. How many seasons did Placido Polanco play in the MLB?

    a. 12
    b. 15
    c. 16
    d. 21

7. Ryan Howard played his entire 13-season MLB career with the Philadelphia Phillies.

    a. True
    b. False

8. Ryne Sandberg spent one season in Philadelphia. Which team did he spend 15 seasons with?

    a. Houston Astros
    b. New York Yankees

    c. Florida Marlins

    d. Chicago Cubs

9. How many All-Star Games was Chase Utley named to in his 16-season career?

    a. 3

    b. 6

    c. 9

    d. 12

10. What year did Scott Rolen win the National League Rookie of the Year Award?

    a. 1996

    b. 1997

    c. 1998

    d. 1999

11. Which Phillies infielder was named the 1980 NLCS MVP?

    a. Manny Trillo

    b. Pete Rose

    c. Larry Bowa

    d. Mike Schmidt

12. Larry Bowa was named the 2001 National League Manager of the Year.

    a. True

    b. False

13. How many MLB All-Star Games was Cookie Rojas named to in his 16-season MLB career?

a. 2

b. 3

c. 5

d. 7

14. What college did former Phillies first baseman Travis Lee attend?

a. Long Beach State University

b. UC Berkeley

c. UC Davis

d. San Diego State University

15. How many Silver Slugger Awards did Chase Utley win during his 16-season MLB career?

a. 2

b. 4

c. 6

d. 8

16. Mike Schmidt was never named National League MVP.

a. True

b. False

17. What was Ryan Howard's batting average for the Phillies' 2008 championship season?

a. .201

b. .231

c. .251

d. .281

18. How many home runs did Jimmy Rollins hit during the Phillies' 2008 championship season?

    a. 11
    b. 22
    c. 33
    d. 44

19. What was Chase Utley's batting average during the Phillies' 2008 championship season?

    a. .280
    b. .287
    c. .292
    d. .332

20. Mike Schmidt hit 48 home runs during the Phillies' 1980 World Championship season.

    a. True
    b. False

QUIZ ANSWERS

1. D – Los Angeles Dodgers

2. A – True

3. C – 46

4. C – 58

5. B – San Diego Padres

6. C – 16

7. A – True

8. D – Chicago Cubs

9. B – 6

10. B – 1997

11. A – Manny Trillo

12. A – True

13. C – 5

14. D – San Diego State University

15. B – 4

16. B – False (He was a 3x MVP.)

17. C – .251

18. A – 11

19. C – .292

20. A – True

DID YOU KNOW?

1. Third baseman Mike Schmidt spent his entire 18-season career with the Philadelphia Phillies. He is a Hall-of-Famer, a 3x MVP, a 12x All-Star, a 1980 World Series Champion, a 10x Gold Glove Award winner, a 6x Silver Slugger Award winner, and a World Series MVP.

2. Second baseman Chase Utley played for the Philadelphia Phillies for 13 seasons and for the Los Angeles Dodgers for four seasons. He is a 6x All-Star, 4x Silver Slugger Award winner, and a 2008 World Series champion.

3. First baseman Ryan Howard spent his entire 13-season career with the Philadelphia Phillies. He is a 3x All-Star, 1x MVP, Rookie of the Year Award winner, Silver Slugger Award winner, NLCS MVP, Major League Player of the Year winner, and 2008 World Series champion.

4. Former Phillie José Bautista was a 6x All-Star and 3x Silver Slugger Award winner. He played for eight MLB teams during his 15-season career. In addition to the Phillies, he played for the Pittsburgh Pirates, Baltimore Orioles, Kansas City Royals, New York Mets, Tampa Bay Devil Rays, Toronto Blue Jays, and the Atlanta Braves.

5. Shortstop Larry Bowa played for the Philadelphia Phillies for 12 seasons, the Chicago Cubs for four seasons, and the New York Mets for one season. He is a

5x All-Star, 2x Gold Glove Award winner, Manager of the Year Award winner, and 1980 World Series Champion.

6. Infielder Dick Allen played for the Philadelphia Phillies for nine seasons, the Chicago White Sox for three seasons, the St. Louis Cardinals for one season, the Oakland A's for one season, and the Los Angeles Dodgers for one season. He is a 7x All-Star, Rookie of the Year Award winner, and 1x MVP.

7. Infielder Placido Polanco played for the Philadelphia Phillies for seven seasons, the St. Louis Cardinals for five seasons, the Detroit Tigers for five seasons, and the Miami Marlins for one season. He is a 2x All-Star, 3x Gold Glove Award winner, Silver Slugger Award winner, and ALCS MVP.

8. Infielder Ryne Sandberg played for the Philadelphia Phillies for one season and the Chicago Cubs for 15 seasons. He is a Hall-of-Famer, 10x All-Star, MVP, 9x Gold Glove Award winner, 7x Silver Slugger Award winner, and Major League Player of the Year.

9. Sparky Anderson spent only one season in MLB as a player. With the Phillies, he played 152 games in 1959 as a second baseman. He went on to be named to the National Baseball Hall of Fame as a manager and was a 2x Manager of the Year Award winner.

10. Former Phillie José Bautista won the 2010 and 2011 American League Hank Aaron Award. This award is given each season to the best hitter in each league.

CHAPTER 12:

PITCHERS AND CATCHERS

QUIZ TIME!

1. What was Steve Carlton's ERA during his 1980 World Series championship season with the Phillies?

    a. 2.04

    b. 2.34

    c. 2.64

    d. 2.84

2. Current Phillies manager Joe Girardi was a catcher during his MLB playing career.

    a. True

    b. False

3. How many All-Star Games was Carlos Ruiz named to in his 12-season career?

    a. 1

    b. 3

    c. 4

    d. 7

4. How many World Series championships did Curt Schilling win in his 20-season MLB career?

   a. 0
   b. 1
   c. 3
   d. 4

5. How many wins did pitcher Roy Halladay collect for the Phillies in 2010?

   a. 16
   b. 18
   c. 21
   d. 22

6. How many shutouts did Cole Hamels pitch as a member of the Phillies?

   a. 4
   b. 5
   c. 6
   d. 7

7. Former Phillies pitcher Robin Roberts was never named to an MLB All-Star Game in his playing career.

   a. True
   b. False

8. How many All-Star Games was former Phillies pitcher Cliff Lee named to in his playing career?

   a. 2
   b. 4

c. 6

d. 8

9. How many strikeouts did A.J. Burnett record with the Phillies in 2008?

    a. 170

    b. 180

    c. 190

    d. 200

10. What year was Jim Bunning named to the National Baseball Hall of Fame?

    a. 1993

    b. 1996

    c. 1997

    d. 1999

11. What was J.A. Happ's ERA for his 2009 season with the Phillies?

    a. 1.85

    b. 2.69

    c. 2.93

    d. 3.18

12. Pitcher Ryan Madson spent his entire 13-year MLB career with the Philadelphia Phillies.

    a. True

    b. False

13. Tug McGraw played for two teams during his 19-season MLB career; the Phillies and which other team?

a. Oakland A's

b. Texas Rangers

c. Los Angeles Dodgers

d. New York Mets

14. How many All-Star Games was former Phillies pitcher Jonathan Papelbon named to during his 12-season career?

    a. 6

    b. 7

    c. 8

    d. 9

15. How many strikeouts did Joe Blanton collect during his 2009 season with the Phillies?

    a. 133

    b. 143

    c. 153

    d. 163

16. Former Blue Jays catcher Mike Lieberthal hit 31 home runs in his 1999 season with the Phillies.

    a. True

    b. False

17. How many Gold Glove Awards did pitcher Jim Kaat win during his 25-season MLB career?

    a. 7

    b. 9

    c. 12

    d. 16

18. During his 19-year MLB career, Robin Roberts pitched for the Phillies, Houston Astros, Chicago Cubs, and

_____.

   a. Oakland A's
   b. New York Mets
   c. Baltimore Orioles
   d. Los Angeles Dodgers

19. How many saves did Brad Lidge collect for the Phillies during their 2008 championship season?

   a. 31
   b. 41
   c. 44
   d. 50

20. Roy Halladay won a Cy Young Award in 2010 as a member of the Philadelphia Phillies.

   a. True
   b. False

QUIZ ANSWERS

1. B – 2.34

2. A – True

3. A – 1

4. C – 3

5. C – 21

6. D – 7

7. B – False (7x All-Star)

8. B – 4

9. C – 190

10. B – 1996

11. C – 2.93

12. B – False (Oakland A's, Washington Nationals, Kansas City Royals, Los Angeles Dodgers)

13. D – New York Mets

14. A – 6

15. D – 163

16. A – True

17. D – 16

18. C – Baltimore Orioles

19. B – 41

20. A – True

DID YOU KNOW?

1. Carlos Ruiz is the only player in the history of the National League to catch four no-hitters and one of only two catchers to do it in MLB history.

2. Pitcher Roy Halladay played for the Philadelphia Phillies for four seasons and for the Toronto Blue Jays for 12 seasons. He is a Hall-of-Famer, 2x Cy Young Award winner, and an 8x All-Star. He also threw a perfect game as a member of the Phillies on May 29, 2010, against the Florida Marlins.

3. Pitcher Steve Carlton played for the Philadelphia Phillies for 15 seasons, the St. Louis Cardinals for seven seasons, the Minnesota Twins for two seasons, and the San Francisco Giants, the Cleveland Indians, and the Chicago White Sox for one season each. He is a Hall-of-Famer, 4x Cy Young Award winner, Triple Crown winner, 10x All-Star, Gold Glove Award winner, ERA title winner, and 2x World Series champion.

4. Pitcher Jim Bunning played for the Philadelphia Phillies for six seasons, the Detroit Tigers for nine seasons, the Pittsburgh Pirates for two seasons, and the Los Angeles Dodgers for one season. He is a Hall-of-Famer and 9x All-Star.

5. Pitcher Curt Schilling played for the Philadelphia Phillies for nine seasons, the Arizona Diamondbacks for

four seasons, the Boston Red Sox for four seasons, the Baltimore Orioles for three seasons, and the Houston Astros for one season. He is a 6x All-Star, World Series MVP, NLCS MVP, and 3x World Series champion.

6. The Phillies have had 13 no-hitters in franchise history. Two of them were perfect games. The no-hitters were thrown by Charles Ferguson, Red Donahue, Chick Fraser, Johnny Lush, Rick Wise, Terry Mulholland, Tommy Greene, Kevin Millwood, Roy Halladay, Cole Hamels/Jake Diekman/Ken Giles/Jonathan Papelbon (combined no-hitter), and Cole Hamels. The two perfect games were thrown by Jim Bunning and Roy Halladay.

7. Pitcher Grover Cleveland Alexander played for the Philadelphia Phillies for eight seasons, the Chicago Cubs for nine seasons, and the St. Louis Cardinals for four seasons. He is a Hall-of-Famer, 3x Triple Crown winner, 5x ERA Title winner, and 1926 World Series champion.

8. Pitcher Robin Roberts played for the Philadelphia Phillies for 14 seasons, the Baltimore Orioles for four seasons, the Houston Astros for two seasons, and the Chicago Cubs for one season. He is a Hall-of-Famer, Major League Player of the Year Award winner, and 7x All-Star.

9. Pitcher Tug McGraw played for the Philadelphia Phillies for 10 seasons and for the New York Mets for nine seasons. He is a 2x All-Star and 2x World Series Champion. His son is also a pretty successful country music artist.

10. Pitcher Cole Hamels has played for the Philadelphia Phillies for 10 seasons, the Texas Rangers for four seasons, and the Chicago Cubs for two seasons. So far, he is a 4x All-Star, NLCS MVP, World Series MVP, and 2008 World Series champion.

CHAPTER 13:

WORLD SERIES

QUIZ TIME!

1. How many World Series have the Philadelphia Phillies won in franchise history?

    a. 0
    b. 1
    c. 2
    d. 4

2. How many NL pennants have the Phillies won?

    a. 3
    b. 5
    c. 7
    d. 9

3. Which team did the Philadelphia Phillies face in the 1980 World Series?

    a. New York Yankees
    b. Oakland Athletics
    c. Minnesota Twins
    d. Kansas City Royals

4. Which team did the Phillies face in the 2008 World Series?

   a. Kansas City Royals
   b. Tampa Bay Rays
   c. Seattle Mariners
   d. Toronto Blue Jays

5. Who was the Phillies' manager during their 1980 World Series win?

   a. Danny Ozark
   b. Dallas Green
   c. Terry Francona
   d. Paul Owens

6. How many games were played in the 1980 World Series?

   a. 4
   b. 5
   c. 6
   d. 7

7. Mike Schmidt was named the 1980 World Series MVP.

   a. True
   b. False

8. Which Phillies player was named the 2008 World Series MVP?

   a. Shane Victorino
   b. Chase Utley
   c. Ryan Howard
   d. Cole Hamels

9. How many games did the 2008 World Series go?

    a. 4

    b. 5

    c. 6

    d. 7

10. Who was the Phillies manager when they won the 2008 World Series?

    a. Charlie Manuel

    b. Ryne Sandberg

    c. Larry Bowa

    d. Terry Francona

11. Which pitcher started Game 1 of the 2008 World Series for the Phillies?

    a. Brett Myers

    b. J.A. Happ

    c. Cole Hamels

    d. Joe Blanton

12. The Philadelphia Phillies lost the 1993 World Series to the Toronto Blue Jays.

    a. True

    b. False

13. Which Phillie hit the most home runs in the 1980 World Series?

    a. Pete Rose

    b. Bob Boone

    c. Bake McBride

    d. Mike Schmidt

14. Which Phillie hit the most home runs in the 2008 World Series?

    a. Chase Utley

    b. Ryan Howard

    c. Carlos Ruiz

    d. Jayson Werth

15. Which of the following Phillies did NOT hit a home run in the 2008 World Series?

    a. Jimmy Rollins

    b. Joe Blanton

    c. Eric Bruntlett

    d. Carlos Ruiz

16. The Philadelphia Phillies have never won a wild card berth.

    a. True

    b. False

17. Which team did the Philadelphia Phillies face in the 1980 NLCS to advance to the World Series?

    a. Florida Marlins

    b. Milwaukee Brewers

    c. Cincinnati Reds

    d. Houston Astros

18. Which team did the Philadelphia Phillies face in the 2008 NLCS to advance to the World Series?

    a. San Francisco Giants

    b. Los Angeles Dodgers

c. Washington Nationals

d. Chicago Cubs

19. What was the final score of Game 6 of the 1980 World Series?

    a. Phillies 9, Royals 6

    b. Phillies 2, Royals 0

    c. Phillies 4, Royals 1

    d. Phillies 8, Royals 4

20. What was the final score of Game 5 of the 2008 World Series?

    a. Phillies 7, Rays 6

    b. Phillies 6, Rays 5

    c. Phillies 5, Rays 4

    d. Phillies 4, Rays 3

QUIZ ANSWERS

1. C – 2

2. C – 7

3. D – Kansas City Royals

4. B – Tampa Bay Rays

5. B – Dallas Green

6. C – 6

7. A – True

8. D – Cole Hamels

9. B – 5

10. A – Charlie Manuel

11. C – Cole Hamels

12. A – True

13. D – Mike Schmidt (2)

14. B – Ryan Howard (3)

15. A – Jimmy Rollins

16. A – True

17. D – Houston Astros

18. B – Los Angeles Dodgers

19. C – Phillies 4, Royals 1

20. D – Phillies 4, Rays 3

DID YOU KNOW?

1. Steve Carlton's 17 strikeouts was the most by any pitcher in the 1980 World Series. Cole Hamels led all Phillies pitchers with 8 strikeouts in the 2008 World Series.

2. Both Taylor Swift and Patti LaBelle sang the National Anthem during the 2008 World Series.

3. Larry Bowa had the most hits for the Phillies in the 1980 World Series with 9 and Jayson Werth led the team in the 2008 World Series with 8 hits.

4. Steve Carlton had the most wins during the 1980 World Series with 2. J.C. Romero had the most wins during the 2008 World Series, also with 2.

5. The 1980 World Series took place from October 14 through October 21. The 2008 World Series took place from October 22 through October 27.

6. Mike Schmidt scored the most runs for the Phillies in the 1980 World Series with 6. Chase Utley scored the most runs for the Phillies in the 2008 World Series with 5.

7. Game 1 of the 1980 World Series was played in Veterans Stadium in Philadelphia. Eddie Sawyer threw out the first pitch and the All-Philadelphia Boys Choir and Mens Choir sang the National Anthem.

8. Game 6 of the 1980 World Series was also played at

Veterans Stadium. Tony Taylor threw out the first pitch and Charley Pride sang the National Anthem.

9. Game 1 of the 2008 World Series was played at Tropicana Field in Tampa, Florida. Bob Stewart threw out the first pitch and the boyband, the Backstreet Boys, sang the National Anthem.

10. Game 5 of the 2008 World Series was played at Citizens Bank Park in Philadelphia. Jim Bunning threw out the first pitch and John Oates from Hall and Oates sang the National Anthem.

CHAPTER 14:

HEATED RIVALRIES

QUIZ TIME!

1. Which team does NOT play in the National League East with the Phillies?

    a. Miami Marlins

    b. New York Mets

    c. Washington Nationals

    d. Baltimore Orioles

2. The Phillies are a founding member of the NL East Division.

    a. True

    b. False

3. Which team did NOT move from the NL East to the NL Central in 1994?

    a. Chicago Cubs

    b. Pittsburgh Pirates

    c. Toronto Blue Jays

    d. St. Louis Cardinals

4. The Phillies have won two World Series. How many have the New York Mets won?

    a. 0
    b. 2
    c. 4
    d. 5

5. The Phillies have won two World Series. How many have the Atlanta Braves won?

    a. 0
    b. 2
    c. 3
    d. 7

6. The Phillies have two World Series. How many have the Pittsburgh Pirates won?

    a. 0
    b. 2
    c. 3
    d. 5

7. The Phillies have won more NL East championships than any other team.

    a. True
    b. False

8. Which player has NOT played for both the Mets and the Phillies?

    a. Joe Blanton
    b. Bobby Abreu

    c. Larry Bowa

    d. Pedro Martinez

9. Which player has NOT played for both the Expos/ Nationals and the Phillies?

    a. Bryce Harper

    b. Howie Kendrick

    c. Pete Rose

    d. Scott Rolen

10. Which player has NOT played for both the Braves and the Phillies?

    a. Terry Mulholland

    b. Jayson Werth

    c. Johnny Oates

    d. Kenny Lofton

11. Which player has NOT played for both the Marlins and the Phillies?

    a. A.J. Burnett

    b. Placido Polanco

    c. Raul Ibañez

    d. Juan Pierre

12. "The City Series" was any series between the Philadelphia Phillies and the Philadelphia Athletics. When the A's moved to Kansas City in 1955, the City Series came to an end.

    a. True

    b. False

13. Which NL East team has NEVER won the NL East Division title?

    a. New York Mets
    b. Florida/Miami Marlins
    c. Montreal Expos/Washington Nationals
    d. Atlanta Braves

14. The NL East and what other division are the only two MLB divisions in which every team has won at least one World Series?

    a. American League West
    b. American League East
    c. American League Central
    d. American League West

15. As of the end of the 2020 season, the last time the Phillies won the division was 2011. When was the last time the New York Mets won the division?

    a. 2010
    b. 2012
    c. 2013
    d. 2015

16. The Montreal Expos won just one National League East title, in 1981.

    a. True
    b. False

17. As of the end of the 2020 season, the last time the Phillies won the division was 2011. When was the last time the Washington Nationals won the division?

a. 2012

b. 2014

c. 2017

d. 2019

18. Which National League East team did the Philadelphia Phillies play in the 1993 NLCS?

    a. Atlanta Braves

    b. New York Mets

    c. Florida Marlins

    d. Montreal Expos

19. The Phillies have two World Series. How many do the Philadelphia/Kansas City/Oakland Athletics have?

    a. 3

    b. 6

    c. 8

    d. 9

20. The Phillies, Mets, and Expos/Nationals are the only founding members that are still in the NL East.

    a. True

    b. False

QUIZ ANSWERS

1. D – Baltimore Orioles

2. A – True

3. C – Toronto Blue Jays

4. B – 2

5. C – 3

6. D – 5

7. B – False (Atlanta Braves have 14; Phillies have second most with 11.)

8. A – Joe Blanton

9. D – Scott Rolen

10. B – Jayson Werth

11. C – Raul Ibañez

12. A – True

13. B – Florida/Miami Marlins

14. C – American League Central

15. D – 2015

16. A – True

17. C – 2017

18. A – Atlanta Braves

19. D – 9

20. A – True (Braves were in NL West until 1994 and Marlins are an expansion team that joined in 1993.)

DID YOU KNOW?

1. From 1969 through 1993, the Philadelphia Phillies and the Pittsburgh Pirates together won more than half of the NL East Division titles (15 out of 25). They were also the only teams in the NL East who won consecutive titles during that span.

2. When the NL Central was created, the Braves were supposed to move and the Pirates were supposed to stay in the NL East. However, the Braves wanted to stay in a division with the Marlins. The Marlins offered to go to the NL Central, but the Pirates ultimately were the ones to change divisions.

3. The Phillies/Nationals rivalry became more ferocious when Bryce Harper decided to sign with the Phillies in 2019 after spending seven seasons in Washington.

4. There was no City Series between the A's and Phillies in 1901 and 1902 due to a legal battle between the National and American Leagues.

5. The Phillies won five consecutive NL East Division titles, from 2007 through 2011.

6. In NL East history, the Atlanta Braves have won the division 14 times, the Phillies 11 times, the Pirates nine times, the Mets six times, the Nationals five times, the Cardinals three times, and the Cubs two times. The Marlins have never won the division.

7. Joe Blanton, Marlon Byrd, Asdrubal Cabrera, Bryce Harper, Howie Kendrick, Brad Lidge, Pedro Martinez, Derrick May, Jonathan Papelbon, Pete Rose, Nate Schierholtz, Matt Stairs, Jayson Werth, and Jerome Williams have all played for both the Phillies and the Expos/Nationals.

8. Bobby Abreu, Rod Barajas, José Bautista, Larry Bowa, Marlon Byrd, Asdrubal Cabrera, Don Cardwell, Lenny Dykstra, Jeff Francoeur, Tug McGraw, and Jason Vargas have all played for both the Phillies and the New York Mets.

9. Peter Bourjos, José Bautista, Michael Bourn, Don Cardwell, Al Dark, Johnny Evers, Jeff Francoeur, Billy Hamilton, Kenny Lofton, Bob Uecker, Terry Mulholland, and Johnny Oates have all played for both the Phillies and the Atlanta Braves.

10. A.J. Burnett, Jeff Francoeur, John Mabry, Logan Morrison, Juan Pierre, Placido Polanco, J.T. Realmuto, Nate Robertson, and Jason Vargas have all played for both the Phillies and the Florida/Miami Marlins.

CHAPTER 15:

THE AWARDS SECTION

QUIZ TIME!

1. Which Phillies pitcher won the National League Cy Young Award in 2010?

   a. Cole Hamels

   b. Roy Halladay

   c. Jamie Moyer

   d. J.A. Happ

2. No Phillies first baseman has ever won a Gold Glove Award.

   a. True

   b. False

3. Which Phillies player won the National League MVP Award in 2007?

   a. Shane Victorino

   b. Chase Utley

   c. Ryan Howard

   d. Jimmy Rollins

4. Which Phillie most recently won the NL Rookie of the Year Award (as of the 2020 season)?

    a. Jack Sanford

    b. Dick Allen

    c. Ryan Howard

    d. Scott Rolen

5. How many NL Gold Glove Awards did Shane Victorino win during his time as a Phillie?

    a. 2

    b. 3

    c. 5

    d. 8

6. Who are the only two third basemen in Phillies franchise history to win Gold Glove Awards?

    a. Mike Schmidt and Scott Rolen

    b. Placido Polanco and Scott Rolen

    c. Mike Schmidt and Placido Polanco

    d. David Bell and Mike Schmidt

7. No Phillies manager has ever won the National League Manager of the Year Award.

    a. True

    b. False

8. Which Phillies player was named the DHL Hometown Hero (voted by MLB fans as the most outstanding player in franchise history)?

    a. Richie Ashburn

    b. Steve Carlton

    c. Robin Roberts

    d. Mike Schmidt

9. Who was the first Phillie named National League Rookie of the Year?

    a. Jack Sanford

    b. Dick Allen

    c. Scott Rolen

    d. Ryan Howard

10. In what year did Pete Rose win his sole Silver Slugger Award?

    a. 1979

    b. 1981

    c. 1982

    d. 1983

11. Which Phillie was named the Wilson MLB Defensive Player of the Year in 2012 and 2013?

    a. Chase Utley

    b. Hunter Pence

    c. Carlos Ruiz

    d. Shane Victorino

12. Jim Thome NEVER won a Silver Slugger Award during his time in Philadelphia.

    a. True

    b. False

13. Who is the only Phillies player ever to win the Hank Aaron Award?

a. Chase Utley

b. Mike Schmidt

c. Jimmy Rollins

d. Ryan Howard

14. Who is the only Phillies hitter ever to win an NL Triple Crown?

a. Chuck Klein

b. Mike Schmidt

c. Pete Rose

d. Scott Rolen

15. Who is the only Phillie ever to win the MLB Heart and Hustle Award?

a. Shane Victorino

b. Cole Hamels

c. Roy Halladay

d. Ryan Howard

16. No Phillies player has ever won the Home Run Derby.

a. True

b. False

17. Who is the only Phillies player ever to win the MLB Comeback Player of the Year Award?

a. J.A. Happ

b. Roy Halladay

c. Brad Lidge

d. Jayson Werth

18. Which of the Phillies listed below NEVER won a Roberto Clemente Award during their time in Philadelphia?

    a. Bobby Abreu
    b. Greg Luzinski
    c. Garry Maddox
    d. Jimmy Rollins

19. How many Gold Glove Awards did Mike Schmidt win in his 18-year career with the Phillies?

    a. 8
    b. 9
    c. 10
    d. 12

20. Former Phillies pitcher Grover Cleveland Alexander won an NL Pitching Triple Crown in back-to-back years, 1915 and 1916.

    a. True
    b. False

QUIZ ANSWERS

1. B – Roy Halladay

2. B – False, Bill White (1966)

3. D – Jimmy Rollins

4. C – Ryan Howard (2005)

5. B – 3

6. A – Mike Schmidt (1976, 1977, 1978, 1979, 1980, 1981, 1982, 1983, 1984, 1986) and Scott Rolen (1998, 2000, 2001)

7. B – False (Larry Bowa in 2001)

8. D – Mike Schmidt

9. A – Jack Sanford (1957)

10. B – 1981

11. C – Carlos Ruiz

12. A – True (He won one in 1996 when he was with the Cleveland Indians.)

13. D – Ryan Howard (2006)

14. A – Chuck Klein (1933)

15. C – Roy Halladay (2010)

16. B – False, Bobby Abreu (2005), Ryan Howard (2006)

17. C – Brad Lidge (2008)

18. A – Bobby Abreu

19. C – 10

20. A – True

DID YOU KNOW?

1. The Philadelphia Phillies have had four different pitchers win Cy Young Awards: Steve Carlton (1972, 1977, 1980, 1982), John Denny (1983), Steve Bedrosian (1987), and Roy Halladay (2010).

2. Jimmy Rollins is the only shortstop in Philadelphia Phillies franchise history ever to win an NL Silver Slugger Award.

3. Four Philadelphia Phillies have won the NL Rookie of the Year Award: Jack Sanford (1957), Dick Allen (1964), Scott Rolen (1997), and Ryan Howard (2005).

4. Roy Halladay won the ESPN ESPY Award for Best Major League Baseball Player in 2011 for his 2010 performance with the Phillies.

5. The Philadelphia Phillies have had five different players win the NL MVP Award: Chuck Klein (1932), Jim Konstanty (1950), Mike Schmidt (1980, 1981, 1986), Ryan Howard (2006), and Jimmy Rollins (2007).

6. Three Phillies players have been named the Rolaids Relief Man of the Year Award: Al Holland (1983), Steve Bedrosian (1987), and Brad Lidge (2008).

7. The only Phillies player ever to win the All-Star Game MVP Award was Johnny Callison in 1964.

8. Five Phillies players have been named NLCS MVP: Manny Trillo (1980), Gary Matthews (1983), Curt

Schilling (1993), Cole Hamels (2008), and Ryan Howard (2009).

9. Although Charlie Manuel is the Phillies' all-time winningest manager, he never won an NL Manager of the Year Award during his time in Philly.

10. The first Phillies player to win a Gold Glove Award was shortstop Bobby Wine in 1963.

CHAPTER 16:

THE CITY OF BROTHERLY LOVE

QUIZ TIME!

1. What was the Liberty Bell originally called?

    a. American Bell

    b. State House Bell

    c. USA Bell

    d. Philly Bell

2. The Walnut Street Theater was originally owned by Edwin Booth, John Wilkes Booth's brother.

    a. True

    b. False

3. Philly is known as what "Capital" of the United States?

    a. Agriculture

    b. Technology

    c. Sandwich

    d. Mural

4. People in Philadelphia consume how many times more pretzels each year, compared to the average American?

    a. 4
    b. 8
    c. 12
    d. 16

5. What percentage of America's population lives within five hours of Philadelphia, and what percentage of Americans live within a two-hour flight of Philadelphia?

    a. 5, 10
    b. 10, 30
    c. 20, 40
    d. 25, 60

6. Eastern State Penitentiary in Philadelphia once held which famous criminal?

    a. Al Capone
    b. "Slick Willie" Sutton
    c. Morris "The Rabbi" Bolber
    d. All of the Above

7. On the Liberty Bell, Pennsylvania is spelled with only one "N."

    a. True
    b. False

8. Which famous actor is from the City of Brotherly Love?

    a. Johnny Depp
    b. Tom Hanks

c. Will Smith

d. Robert Downey Jr.

9. What is the name of Philadelphia's NFL team?

a. Philadelphia Eagles

b. Philadelphia Chargers

c. Philadelphia Cardinals

d. Philadelphia Patriots

10. What is the name of Philadelphia's NBA team?

a. Philadelphia Heat

b. Philadelphia Warriors

c. Philadelphia Magic

d. Philadelphia 76ers

11. What is the name of Philadelphia's NHL team?

a. Philadelphia Kings

b. Philadelphia Penguins

c. Philadelphia Flyers

d. Philadelphia Lightning

12. Philadelphia's MLS team is called the Philadelphia Union.

a. True

b. False

13. Where in Philadelphia were the Declaration of Independence and the Constitution signed?

a. Philadelphia City Hall

b. Christ Church

c. Independence Hall

d. One Liberty Place

14. What building's steps were immortalized in the run up the stairs scene in the film "Rocky"?

    a. Philadelphia Museum of Art

    b. Independence Hall

    c. The Franklin Institute

    d. Rodin Museum

15. What is the name of the arena that the Philadelphia 76ers of the NBA and the Philadelphia Flyers of the NHL call home?

    a. Pepsi Center

    b. Wells Fargo Center

    c. United Center

    d. Smoothie King Center

16. What is the name of the stadium that the Philadelphia Eagles of the NFL call home?

    a. Lincoln Financial Field

    b. Nissan Stadium

    c. Ford Field

    d. Hard Rock Stadium

17. Which famous basketball player was born in Philadelphia?

    a. Lebron James

    b. Kobe Bryant

    c. Steph Curry

    d. Shaquille O' Neal

18. Philadelphia International Airport is 5 miles away from Citizens Bank Park. What is the Philadelphia International Airport's code?

    a. PHD
    b. PIA
    c. PIL
    d. PHL

19. One out of every how many doctors in the United States is trained in Philadelphia?

    a. 3
    b. 6
    c. 8
    d. 10

20. Central High School in Philadelphia is the only high school in America that can grant bachelor's degrees to its students.

    a. True
    b. False

QUIZ ANSWERS

1. B – State House Bell

2. A – True

3. D – Mural

4. C – 12

5. D – 25, 60

6. D – All of the Above

7. A – True

8. C – Will Smith

9. A – Philadelphia Eagles

10. D – Philadelphia 76ers

11. C – Philadelphia Flyers

12. A – True

13. C – Independence Hall

14. A – Philadelphia Museum of Art

15. B – Wells Fargo Center

16. A – Lincoln Financial Field

17. B – Kobe Bryant

18. D – PHL

19. B – 6

20. A – True

DID YOU KNOW?

1. Philadelphia was home to the first hospital, medical school, zoo, newspaper, soft pretzel, lager beer, cheesesteak, lending library, fire company, first naval shipyard in America, first mint in America, and the first general-use computer.

2. The first Republican National Convention was held at Philadelphia's Musical Fund Hall in June of 1856.

3. Bartram's Garden is the oldest botanical garden in North America. The Penn Museum is home to the largest Egyptian Sphynx in the Western Hemisphere.

4. The Mütter Museum is home to several oddities, including slices of Albert Einstein's brain, tissue from the body of John Wilkes Booth, a corpse that turned into soap, and a tumor removed from President Grover Cleveland.

5. As an April Fool's Day prank in 1996, Taco Bell took out a full-page ad in six major newspapers claiming they had purchased the Liberty Bell and renamed it the "Taco Liberty Bell." People were outraged, to say the least.... April Fool's!

6. "In West Philadelphia born and raised, On the playground is where I spent most of my days Chilling out, maxing, relaxing all cool and all shooting some b-

ball outside of the school, When a couple of guys who were up to no good started making trouble in my neighborhood I got in one little fight and my mom got scared and said "You're moving with your auntie and uncle in Bel-Air" – Lyrics to *The Fresh Prince of Bel-Air* theme song

7. The famous Philly Cheesesteak was created in 1930 by Pat Olivieri, who owned a hot dog stand. According to his grandnephew, the current owner of Pat's King of Steaks, it originally did not even have cheese on it. It was originally steak and onions on a hot dog bun. The provolone cheese was an addition a little over a decade later.

8. Around 50 tree seedlings traveled to space with the Apollo 14 mission. One of these "moon trees" was planted in Philly's Washington Square Park. When the tree began to die in 2011, the National Park Service replaced it with a clone.

9. Philadelphia is home to more impressionist paintings than any other city in the world, besides Paris. Philly also has a Rodin Museum, which makes the city the largest collector of the sculptor's work outside of Paris.

10. Of the 100 questions on the United States Citizenship Test, half of the answers can be found in Philadelphia. The city is like one huge American history lesson.

CHAPTER 17:

LEFTY

QUIZ TIME!

1. Where was Steve Carlton born?

    a. San Diego, California

    b. Miami, Florida

    c. Denver, Colorado

    d. Indianapolis, Indiana

2. Steve Carlton's full name is Steven Norman Carlton.

    a. True

    b. False

3. Steve Carlton played for the Philadelphia Phillies for 15 of the 24 seasons he was in MLB. He also played for the St. Louis Cardinals, Minnesota Twins, San Francisco Giants, Cleveland Indians, and which other team?

    a. San Diego Padres

    b. Chicago White Sox

    c. Florida Marlins

    d. Kansas City Royals

4. What year was Steve Carlton born?

    a. 1949

    b. 1947

    c. 1945

    d. 1944

5. What uniform number did Steve Carlton wear as a member of the Phillies?

    a. 32

    b. 34

    c. 36

    d. 38

6. How many strikeouts did Steve Carlton record during his 24 MLB seasons?

    a. 3,990

    b. 4,001

    c. 4,136

    d. 4,583

7. Steve Carlton NEVER threw a no-hitter.

    a. True

    b. False

8. Steve Carlton is a 2x World Series Champion. He won a title in 1980 with the Phillies and another in 1967 with which team?

    a. Minnesota Twins

    b. Cleveland Indians

    c. St. Louis Cardinals

    d. Chicago White Sox

9. What college did Steve Carlton attend?

    a. Florida State University

    b. Miami Dade College

    c. University of Florida

    d. University of Miami

10. How many All-Star Games was Steve Carlton named to?

    a. 10

    b. 13

    c. 18

    d. 21

11. How many Gold Glove Awards did Steve Carlton win?

    a. 9

    b. 3

    c. 1

    d. 0

12. Steve Carlton committed 90 balks in his career, the most in MLB history.

    a. True

    b. False

13. What year was Steve Carlton inducted into the National Baseball Hall of Fame with 95.82% of the vote?

    a. 1993

    b. 1994

    c. 1995

    d. 1996

14. What year did Steve Carlton win a Pitching Triple Crown?

    a. 1970
    b. 1972
    c. 1974
    d. 1976

15. How many National League Cy Young Awards did Steve Carlton win?

    a. 1
    b. 2
    c. 3
    d. 4

16. Steve Carlton was the National League ERA leader in 1972.

    a. True
    b. False

17. How many times did Steve Carlton lead the National League in wins?

    a. 1
    b. 3
    c. 4
    d. 7

18. How many times Steve Carlton lead the National League in strikeouts?

    a. 1
    b. 3

c. 4

d. 5

19. What year did the Phillies retire Steve Carlton's No. 32?

    a. 1987

    b. 1989

    c. 1994

    d. 1998

20. In 2004, the Phillies unveiled a statue of Steve Carlton at Citizens Bank Park.

    a. True

    b. False

QUIZ ANSWERS

1. B – Miami, Florida

2. A – True

3. B – Chicago White Sox

4. D -1944

5. A – 32

6. C – 4,136

7. A – True

8. C – St. Louis Cardinals

9. B – Miami Dade College

10. A – 10

11. C – 1 (1981)

12. A – True

13. B – 1994

14. B – 1972

15. D – 4

16. A – True

17. C – 4 (1972, 1977, 1980, 1982)

18. D – 5 (1972, 1974, 1980, 1982, 1983)

19. B – 1989

20. A – True

DID YOU KNOW?

1. Steve Carlton has the most career strikeouts and the second-most career wins for any left-handed pitcher in MLB history.

2. Steve Carlton threw a whopping 30 complete games in his 1972 season with the Phillies. His ERA that year was 1.97 and he won 27 games. This was his first season in Philadelphia. He led the league in wins, ERA, innings pitched, and strikeouts. He also won his first Cy Young Award this season.

3. "Lefty was a craftsman, an artist. He was a perfectionist. He painted a ballgame. Stroke, stroke, stroke, and when he got through, it was a masterpiece." – Richie Ashburn

4. Steve Carlton made his MLB debut against the Chicago Cubs and played his final game against the Cleveland Indians.

5. Steve Carlton finished his career with a 329-244 record. His career ERA was 3.22. He appeared in 741 games, started 709 of them, earned 2 saves, and pitched a total of 5,217.2 innings.

6. Steve Carlton got the win in both Game 2 and Game 6 of the 1980 World Series. He pitched 15 innings, gave up 14 hits, struck out 17, and gave up 4 earned runs in his two starts.

7. Steve Carlton one struck out 19 Mets batters in one game…. and lost.

8. Carlton appeared in an episode of *Married… with Children*. He played himself.

9. "Why do you think you were put on this earth?" – ESPN's Roy Firestone

   "To teach the world how to throw a slider." – Steve Carlton's response

10. "Trying to get a hit off of Carlton is] like trying to drink coffee with a fork" – Hall-of-Famer Willie Stargell

CHAPTER 18:

J – ROLL

QUIZ TIME!

1. Where was Jimmy Rollins born?

    a. Madison, Wisconsin

    b. Philadelphia, Pennsylvania

    c. Detroit, Michigan

    d. Oakland, California

2. Jimmy Rollins is the cousin of Tony Tarasco, who played in the majors from 1993 to 2002.

    a. True

    b. False

3. Jimmy Rollins played for three teams during his 17-season MLB career: the Phillies, the Chicago White Sox, and which other team?

    a. Washington Nationals

    b. St. Louis Cardinals

    c. Los Angeles Dodgers

    d. Oakland Athletics

4. What year was Jimmy Rollins born?

   a. 1975
   b. 1978
   c. 1980
   d. 1983

5. How many MLB All-Star Games was Jimmy Rollins named?

   a. 3
   b. 6
   c. 7
   d. 10

6. What year was Jimmy Rollins named the National League MVP?

   a. 2001
   b. 2003
   c. 2005
   d. 2007

7. Jimmy Rollins appeared in several MC Hammer music videos when he was young.

   a. True
   b. False

8. How many Gold Glove Awards did Jimmy Rollins win?

   a. 2
   b. 4
   c. 8
   d. 12

9. What year did Jimmy Rollins win his sole Silver Slugger Award?

    a. 2005
    b. 2006
    c. 2007
    d. 2008

10. What MLB team was Jimmy Rollins a fan of when he was growing up?

    a. Philadelphia Phillies
    b. San Francisco Giants
    c. Los Angeles Dodgers
    d. Oakland A's

11. In what year did Jimmy Rollins win a Roberto Clemente Award?

    a. 2011
    b. 2012
    c. 2014
    d. 2015

12. Jimmy Rollins spent 15 out of the 17 seasons of his MLB career with the Philadelphia Phillies.

    a. True
    b. False

13. How many career home runs did Jimmy Rollins hit?

    a. 201
    b. 231
    c. 281
    d. 301

14. What year did Jimmy Rollins lead the National League in stolen bases?

    a. 2001
    b. 2005
    c. 2008
    d. 2011

15. How many stolen bases did Jimmy Rollins collect during the 2001 season?

    a. 31
    b. 36
    c. 46
    d. 50

16. Jimmy Rollins won the 2001 NL Rookie of the Year Award.

    a. True
    b. False

17. How many games did Jimmy Rollins play in for the Phillies during the 2007 season?

    a. 150
    b. 155
    c. 160
    d. 162

18. What is Jimmy Rollins' full name?

    a. Rutherford James Rollins
    b. Timothy James Rollins
    c. James Peter Rollins
    d. James Calvin Rollins

19. In his MLB debut, Rollins played against the Florida Marlins. His final game in the MLB was against the

_____.

  a. Arizona Diamondbacks
  b. Milwaukee Brewers
  c. Washington Nationals
  d. Colorado Rockies

20. Jimmy Rollins retained his role as the Phillies' leadoff hitter for almost a full decade.

  a. True
  b. False

QUIZ ANSWERS

1. D – Oakland, California

2. A – True

3. C – Los Angeles Dodgers

4. B – 1978

5. A – 3

6. D – 2007

7. A – True

8. B – 4

9. C – 2007

10. D – Oakland A's

11. C – 2014

12. A – True

13. B – 231

14. A – 2001

15. C – 46

16. B – False (He came in 3rd; Albert Pujols won the award.)

17. D – 162

18. D – James Calvin Rollins

19. C – Washington Nationals

20. A – True

DID YOU KNOW?

1. In 2019, the Phillies hired Jimmy Rollins as a special advisor to the team. He was also an on-air commentator for a few Phillies games. He was honored in 2019 with a retirement ceremony. Although his No. 11 is not formally retired by the Phillies, they do keep it out of rotation in his honor.

2. Jimmy and his wife Johari established the Johari and Jimmy Rollins Center for Animal Rehabilitation in New Jersey. It offers rehab services and medical help to animals in need.

3. Jimmy Rollins holds an annual BaseBowl charity bowling tournament with proceeds benefitting the Arthritis Foundation.

4. Jimmy Rollins actively campaigned for Barack Obama in the 2008 election.

5. Jimmy Rollins is an investor in the eSports company, NRG Esports. Other NRG Esports investors include Alex Rodriguez, Ryan Howard, Shaquille O' Neal, Michael Strahan, Marshawn Lynch, and Jennifer Lopez.

6. In 2016, Jimmy Rollins signed a minor-league contract with the San Francisco Giants but was released right before the season began.

7. Jimmy Rollins admired Rickey Henderson while

growing up and tried to emulate him at the plate and in the way in which he played the game.

8. In 2014, Jimmy Rollins was traded from the Phillies to the Los Angeles Dodgers. Rollins waived his no-trade clause to make the move possible.

9. Jimmy Rollins was the first Phillies shortstop to win a Gold Glove Award since Larry Bowa in 1978.

10. Jimmy Rollins was the first player in MLB history to record 200 hits, 30 home runs, 20 triples, and 30 stolen bases in a single season.

CONCLUSION

Learn anything new? Now you truly are the ultimate Phillies fan! Not only did you learn about the Phillies of the modern era but you also expanded your knowledge back to the days of the 1980 and 2008 World Series championships.

You learned about the Phillies' origins, their history, and where they came from. You learned about the history of their uniforms and jersey numbers, you identified some famous quotes, and read some of the craziest nicknames of all time. You learned more about powerhouse hitter, Mike "Schmitty" Schmidt, Steve "Lefty" Carlton, and Jimmy "J-Roll" Rollins. You were amazed by Phillies stats and recalled some of the most famous Phillies trades and drafts/draft picks of all time. You broke down your knowledge by outfielders, infielders, pitchers, and catchers. You looked back on the Phillies championships and playoff feats and the awards that came before, after, and during them. You also learned about the Phillies' fiercest rivalries both within and outside their division.

Every team in the MLB has a storied history, but the Phillies have one of the most memorable of all. They have won two incredible World Series championships with the backing of their devoted fans. Being the ultimate Phillies fan takes knowledge and a whole lot of patience, which you tested with this book. Whether you knew every answer or were stumped by several questions, you learned some of the most interesting history that the game of baseball has to offer.

The history of the Phillies represents what we all love about the game of baseball. The heart, the determination, the tough times, and the unexpected moments, plus the players that inspire us and encourage us to do our best because, even if you get knocked down, there is always another game and another day.

With players like Bryce Harper, Andrew McCutchen, and Jake Arrieta, the future for the Phillies continues to look bright. There is no doubt that this franchise will continue to be one of the most competitive teams in Major League Baseball year after year.

It's a new decade, which means there is a clean slate, ready to continue writing the history of the Philadelphia Phillies. The ultimate Phillies fans cannot wait to see what's to come for their beloved Phils.

You are a reporter for the Star. It is a Tuesday morning
in October of this year. An employe of the Litton Mortuary comes into office and hands you obituary form and
photo of deceased person. Form contains following information:

Name: Robert G. Quigley. Resided at: 1227 N. Clay.
Died, when: Last night at 9:30. Where: Jonesville
General Hospital. Cause of death: Heart disease. Length
of illness, remarks: Three months. Became seriously ill
week ago; taken to hospital then.

Date and place of birth: July 6, 1933, Hobart. Parents'
names: Mr. and Mrs. Harold C. Quigley. Marriage, date
and place: June 10, 1958, Hobart. To whom: Sarah
Henderson of Hobart. Places of residence: Hobart until
1957; Jonesville since 1957.

Education: Hobart High School, 1951; B.A. degree, Dexter,
1957. Occupation: Employe of Colton Department Store
since 1957; promoted to assistant manager, 1964; to manager, 1970. Remarks: U.S. Army, Korean War, 1951-53.

Affiliations, activities: Member, Woodview Baptist
church; member, Rotary Club, president, 1968; member,
Chamber of Commerce.

Survivors: Widow; son, Arthur T., and daughter, Judith,
both at home; mother, Mrs. Harold C. Quigley, Hobart;
brothers, Richard E., Hobart, and Orville B., Grossboro;
sister, Mrs. Frank L. Barnes, Hobart.

Mortuary: Litton Mortuary in charge. Funeral services,
where: Woodview Baptist church. When: Thursday, 2 p.m.
Minister: Rev. Albert Foster. Interment: Roselawn cemetary,
Jonesville.

You wish to verify the facts and names, particularly the

names of the survivors, so you phone the family. You are
told that Mr. Quigley was a member of Butler Post No. 45,
American Legion.

It's a Tuesday morning in August. You are a reporter for
the Star, making telephone check of General Hospital.

You are told that Arthur L. Eldredge died at 8:30 this
morning. Heart disease. Patient in hospital 10 days.
Faculty member at Dexter University. Body at Litton
Mortuary.

You call Litton Mortuary. An employe says he will come
to Star office with information in about an hour. Mortuary
employe later comes in with obituary blank containing
this information:

Name: Arthur L. Eldredge. Resided at: 1104 W. Texas.
Died, when: 8:30 a.m. today. Where: Jonesville General
Hospital. Cause of death: Heart disease. Length of
illness, remarks: Ill four months. Suffered severe
heart attack at home 10 days ago and was taken to
hospital.

Date and place of birth: June 28, 1918, Concord, Mich.
Parents' names: George T. and Harriet A. Eldredge.
Marriage, date and place: June 12, 1946, Marshall,
Mich. To whom: Barbara Edith White of Marshall.

Education: Graduate, Concord High School, 1936. Attended Hillsdale College, Hillsdale, Mich., 1937-41, B.A.
degree, 1941; M.A. degree, U. of Michigan, 1947; Ph.D.
degree, U. of Mich., 1953. Remarks: U.S. Army, 1941-45.

Occupation: Worked in department store in Concord one
year, 1936-37; instructor, Olivet College, Olivet, Mich.,
1947-49; instructor, U. of Michigan, 1949-54; joined
faculty, Dexter, as asst. professor of history, 1954;
appointed dean of men, 1968.

Affiliations, activities: Member of Phi Beta Kappa,
honorary scholastic fraternity; member of American

63

Historical Association; member of Jonesville Exchange
Club, president, 1962; member of local Masonic Lodge;
chairman, professional division, United Fund campaign,
last year; member, Woodview Baptist Church.

Remarks: Listed in Who's Who in America. Author of
History of the Southwest. Also author of about a
dozen short stories on the Old West, published in
several magazines.

Survivors: Widow; son, Harold R., Philadelphia;
daughter, Mrs. Fred T. Johnson, Baltimore; two
brothers, Francis P. Eldredge, Grand Rapids, Mich.,
Arnold T., Detroit; sister, Mrs. Charles E. Dutton,
Chicago; three grandchildren.

Mortuary in charge: Litton Mortuary. Funeral services,
where: Woodview Baptist church. When: Friday, 2 p.m.
Minister: Rev. Alfred Foster. Burial: Roselawn
cemetery, Jonesville.

You are a reporter for the Star. It's a Monday morning
in October and you check Jonesville General Hospital by
phone. You are told that Francis P. Civella died in
hospital this morning at 2:30. Body taken to Perry
Funeral Home.

You call the funeral home and are given this information:

Name: Francis P. Civella. Resided at: 2904 E. Rose.
Died, when: 2:30 a.m. today. Where: Jonesville General
Hospital. Cause of Death: Heart disease. Length of
illness, remarks: 2 years. Became worse 3 weeks ago,
taken to hospital at that time.

Date and place of birth: Apr. 4, 1925, Jonesville.
Parents' names: Mr. and Mrs. Paul E. Civella. Marriage,
date and place: June 12, 1950, Jonesville. To whom:
Constance Mason of Jonesville.

Education: Graduate, Central High School, 1943; attended
Dexter, 1946-50; B.A. degree, 1950; master's degree,
Dexter, 1956.

Occupation: Teacher; Central High school, 1950 until his
death.

Affiliations, activities: Member, St. Joseph Catholic
Church; member, Exchange Club. Hobby, stamp collecting.
Active worker, United Fund, since 1955.

Remarks: Enlisted in Army, June, 1943; served until April
1946.

Survivors: Widow; son, John, and daughter, Mary, both
at home; sister, Mrs. Frank T. Johnson, Madison; brother,
Frederick, Philadelphia.

Mortuary in charge: Perry Funeral Home. Funeral services,

where: St. Joseph Catholic Church. When: Mass,
Thursday, 10 a.m. Minister: Rev. Thomas A. Murphy.
Burial: church cemetery.

You are a reporter for the Star. It's a Wednesday
morning in May of this year. An employe of Perry Funeral
Home comes into office and hands you obituary form and
recent photo of deceased person. Form contains the
following information:

Name: Harry C. Colton. Resided at: 1529 S. Clay St.
Died, when: Last night at 10:15. Where: Jonesville
General hospital. Cause of death: Heart disease.
Length of illness, remarks: Five months. Suffered
a severe heart attack at his home two weeks ago and was
taken to hospital.

Date and place of birth: Feb. 17, 1899, Jonesville.
Parents' names: John C. and Marie Harper Colton.
Marriage, date and place: Jonesville, June 12, 1928.
To whom: Rose Mary Paige of Jonesville. Places of
residence: Lifelong resident of Jonesville.

Education: Central High school, Jonesville, 1917;
attended Dexter U. two years, 1919-21.

Occupation: Employe, Smallwood Department Store, 1921-
37; manager of men's wear department, 1928-37. Founded
Colton Department Store, 1937; president since that time.
Store first located in 200 block of N. Clay; moved to
present, larger quarters, 1948.

Affiliations, activities: Member, First Presbyterian church;
Rotary club; member, Chamber of Commerce, president, 1944;
Butler Post No. 45, American Legion; Jonesville Country
Club; member, board of directors, Jonesville Manufacturing
co.; member, board of directors, City National Bank;
member, State Retail Dealers Association, vice president,
1947; member, County Board of Supervisers, since 1958.

Remarks: Army, June, 1917, to Dec. 1918, World War I;
overseas, eight months.

Survivors: Widow; son, John D., Grossville; son, Charles E., Salem; daughter, Mrs. William R. Johnston, Bradley; brother, Francis C. Colton, Salem; sister, Mrs. Norman J. Decker, Jonesville; four grandchildren.

Mortuary in charge: Perry Funeral Home. Funeral services, where: First Presbyterian Church. When: Friday afternoon, 2 p.m. Minister: Rev. Joseph L. Dickerson. Burial: Roselawn Cemetery (Jonesville).

You wish to verify some of facts and names, particularly those of survivors, so you phone family. A member of family says Mr. Colton was gun collector. One of best collections of antique guns in the state. Also says he was former commander of Legion Post and former state Legion officer, but not certain when. You phone an officer of post. Colton commander of local post, 1938; state vice commander, 1939.

Write the story for today's Star.

You are a reporter for the Sun. It's a Tuesday evening
in April of this year. Employe of Perry Funeral Home
comes into office and hands you obituary form and recent
photo of deceased person. The form contains following
information:

Name: Phillip V. Richardson. Resided at: 405 Forest.
Died, when: Today at 3:45 p.m. Where: Jonesville
General Hospital. Cause of death: Cancer. Length of
illness, remarks: Eight months; condition became serious,
taken to hospital two weeks ago. Working until two
months ago.

Date and Place of birth: July 10, 1907, Albion.
Parents: Harry T. and Martha Martin Richardson. Marriage,
date and place: June 9, 1930, Albion. To whom: Louise
Corrinne Appleton of Albion.

Education: Graduate, Albion HS, 1925; graduate, Dexter,
bachelor's degree in engineering, 1929.

Occupation: Employe, city engineer's office, 1929-36;
established Richardson Construction Co., 1936, president
since that time.

Affiliations, activities: Member, Grace Methodist church;
member, Exchange club, president, 1956; member, Chamber
of Commerce; member, board of directors, City National
bank; member of Jonesville Engineering society, president,
1952; member, County Board of Supervisors, 1954-58;
member, State Engineering Society, vice president, 1959.

Remarks: Chairman, industrial division, United Fund campaign, 1964. Has spoken at several engineering conferences
sponsored by College of Engineering, Dexter U.

Survivors: Widow; son, John C. Richardson, Shelby; son,
Alfred D. Richardson, Huntertown; daughter, Mrs. Frederick

R. Porter, Albion; daughter, Mrs. Glen H. Perkins,
Jonesville; brothers, Samuel E. and Harry C. Richardson,
Albion; brother, Homer W. Richardson, Gilead; sisters,
Mrs. Maurice D. Johnson, Erie, Mrs. Carleton P. Adams,
Albion; five grandchildren.

Mortuary in charge: Perry Funeral home. Funeral services,
where: Grace Methodist church. When: Thursday afternoon,
2 o'clock. Minister: Rev. James G. Ballard. Burial:
Roselawn cemetery, Jonesville. Pall bearers: Edward
W. Kramer, Henry C. Boling, Norman A. Decker, Alfred G.
Gaines, Howard C. Greene, Fred E. Ruston, all of
Jonesville.

You wish to verify some of facts and names, particularly
those of survivors, so you phone the family. A member
of family says that Mr. Richardson was president of
Dexter Alumni association in 1957.

Write the story for tomorrow morning's Sun.

31 / STAIRS FALL

You are a reporter for the afternoon Star. You make your
regular phone check of General Hospital at about 8 a.m.
and you are told that Chester B. Miller, 324 East Zinnia
Ave., was admitted unconscious at about 7 this morning.
Had fallen in his home.

You handle some rewrites, check other news sources on your
beat and write several stories. At 9:30 you phone hospital
again. Miller died at 8:15. Skull fracture. Never
regained consciousness. Body has been taken to Perry
Funeral Home.

You phone funeral home. Funeral home employe says he
doesn't have information complete yet, but should have
it ready soon. He will call you back within 15 minutes.
You then phone Police Station. You ask who is investi-
gating Miller death; desk sergeant says it's Officer Fred
C. Denham. Says Denham hasn't returned, but should do
so soon. Desk sergeant suggests that you call back in
about 20 minutes.

Funeral home employe calls, gives you this biographical
data about Miller:

Date of birth: Aug. 26, 1922. Place of birth: Jonesville.
Son of Mr. and Mrs. Wallace E. Miller. Graduated, Central
HS, 1940. B.A. degree, Dexter, 1947. Accountant with
Humble, 1958-65. Office manager, Humble, since 1965.
Formerly employed by Ruston Insurance company. Member,
Grace Methodist church, Masonic lodge, Exchange Club.
Survivors: widow; son, Fred B. Miller, Indianapolis;
daughter, Mrs. William C. Johnson, Shelby; two brothers,
Phillip D. Miller, Baltimore, and Bruce J. Miller,
Philadelphia; one sister, Mrs. Harry J. Ashley, Jonesville;
four grandchildren. Funeral arrangements not complete.

Then you call Police Station again. Officer Denham has
returned; he reports on his investigation at Miller residence.

71

Says Mrs. Miller told him she got up shortly after 6 and
went downstairs to prepare breakfast. At about 6:30 she
called to her husband and told him breakfast was ready.
He answered, said he would be right down. Mrs. Miller
heard husband moving about upstairs. Heard him start
down stairs; then heard him fall. She rushed into living
room. Mr. Miller apparently tripped near top of stairs.
When Mrs. Miller reached her husband, he was unconscious.
She didn't try to move him but called hospital and an
ambulance was sent to take Mr. Miller to hospital.

Then you call coroner. Dr. Klein says he has investigated accident; says no inquest will be necessary.

Write story for today's paper.

You are police reporter for the Sun. It's a Monday afternoon in June; you stop at Police Station to make news
check. Desk sergeant says a Mr. Kane fell from ladder
and was taken to hospital. You check report and find man
involved is Philip S. Kane, 427 Eaton st. On ladder
painting his house. Fell; unconscious. Happened at about
2 p.m. today. Mrs. Kane was in yard, taking clothes off
line. Stray dog was chasing a cat. Cat ran along house,
under ladder. Dog bumped ladder; Mr. Kane lost balance
and fell. Had started painting house this morning. Taken
to Jonesville General hospital in police ambulance.

It's about 4:30. You call hospital. You are told he is
still unconscious; never regained consciousness since
brought to hospital; skull fracture and internal injuries;
condition critical. You again call hospital at 8. You're
told Mr. Kane died at 7:15; never conscious while in
hospital. Body taken to Perry Funeral home. Some time
later employe of funeral home brings in obituary blank
with following information:

Name: Philip S. Kane. Resided at: 427 Eaton st.
Died, when: Today, 7:15 p.m. Where: Jonesville General
hospital. Cause of death: Skull fracture, internal
injuries. Length of illness, remarks: Fell from ladder
today at about 2 p.m.

Date and place of birth: July 10, 1935 , Shelby. Parents'
names: Mr. and Mrs. Paul S. Kane. Marriage,date and
place: June 16, 1959, Shelby. To whom: Sarah Sanderson
of Shelby.

Education: Graduated, Shelby HS, 1953. A.B. degree, Dexter,
1957. Occupation: teacher, Bradford Elementary School,
1957-64; appointed principle of Bradford, 1964.

Affiliations, activities: Member, Grace Methodist church;
member, Exchange club; scoutmaster, Boy Scout Troop No.
12. Member of debate team while student at Dexter.

Remarks: Graduated magna cum laude at Dexter.

Survivors: Widow; two children, Fred and Elizabeth, at
home; parents, Mr. and Mrs. Paul S. Kane, Shelby; two
brothers, Harold E., Shelby, and Arnold B., Erie; sister,
Mrs. Frederick L. Williams, Shelby.

Mortuary in charge: Perry Funeral Home. Funeral services,
where: Grace Methodist church. When: Thursday, 1:30 p.m.
Minister: Rev. James D. Ballard. Burial: River View
cemetery, Shelby.

You phone county coroner. He says inquest not necessary.

74

33 / TREE FALL

You're the police reporter for the Sun; your beat includes hospitals. It is Wednesday afternoon late in June. You check Jonesville General Hospital and you're told a boy has been admitted; injuried in fall from tree.

His name is Paul B. Kelley, 10 years old, son of Mr. and Mrs. Alfred T. Kelley, 421 S. Lincoln. Condition critical. Brought to hospital in police ambulance.

You go to police station to make your regular call and to check this story out. You find that Patrolman Ralph E. Brannon investigated accident. He tells you Paul and friend were flying Paul's kite in vacant lot. Lot is in 400 block of S. Lincoln. You ask who friend was and you're told it was Fred C. Sanson, son of Mr. and Mrs. Norman A. Sanson, 507 S. Lincoln.

Kite came down, was caught in tree near front of lot. Paul climbed tree to get kite; Fred stayed on the ground. Fred told Brannon Paul had reached kite; he was getting it loose from tree limb; lost his footing, fell. Landed on sidewalk. You ask how high boy was. Brannon says about 25 feet. Landed on hand and arm, then head hit sidewalk.

Brannon says Fred ran to Kelley house and told Mrs. Kelley. She ran across street to vacant lot; Paul unconscious on ground. Neighbor called police; ambulance took him to hospital. You ask Brannon when this happened. He says about 10:30 this morning.

You return to Sun office and write some other police-beat stories. It's now 5:45 p.m. and you call hospital again. Paul died at 5:10 p.m. Had broken right arm and skull fracture. Body was taken to Perry Funeral Home.

You call Sanson home. Fred is upset; you talk to Mrs. Sanson. Fred is 10 years old. Classmate of Paul at Lampton Elementary school. Both in 4th grade this past year.

75

Later in evening you check Perry Funeral home. You are
told Paul was born in Jonesville; was 10 last March 14.
He was a Cub Scout. Surviving: Parents; brother John;
sister Marie, both at home; grandparents, Mr. and Mrs.
Frank B. Kelley, Trenton, Mr. and Mrs. Homer E. Johnston,
Warren.

Funeral services, Perry Funeral home Friday, 2 p.m. Rev.
Alfred Foster of Woodview Baptist church will officiate.
Burial, Roselawn Cemetary, Jonesville.

You are a reporter for the Sun. It's a Tuesday afternoon in late June. You are covering your police beat.
You see report that Bruce E. McDonald fell and was taken
in police ambulance to Jonesville General hospital. At
about 5:30 p.m. you call hospital. You are told McDonald
died at 4 p.m. Had skull fracture. Body taken to Litton
Mortuary.

You call police and talk to officer who investigated,
Patrolman Edward B. Kelly. He says accident happened
at about 7 a.m. McDonald going down front steps; to
get morning newspaper lying in yard. Stepped on baseball bat; bat belonged to son, Fred. McDonald fell,
struck head on bottom step. Came back into house. Told
wife what had happened. Told her he had severe headache.
Lay on davenport; about 8 o'clock, became unconscious.
Ambulance was called. McDonald never regained consciousness.
Resided at 204 Charles st.

Litton Mortuary furnishes this information: Born, Apr.
10, 1929, in Shelby. Parents, Mr. and Mrs. Henry R.
McDonald. Married, Mae Miller of Shelby June 14, 1958.
Graduate, Shelby H.S., 1947, Dexter Univ., 1951, B.S.
degree in electrical engineering. Two years in Army,
Korean War. Began working for Robertson Electric Co.,
1953. Became manager, 1963. Member, Grace Methodist
Church, Exchange club.

Survivors: Parents, in Shelby; wife; children, Mary and
Fred, both at home. Funeral, Friday 2 p.m., Grace Methodist
church. Rev. James E. Ballard to conduct services. Burial,
Roselawn cemetery. Litton Mortuary in charge.

You are a reporter for the Star making first check of
your beat and phone the Jonesville General Hospital.
It's about 8 a.m. on a Tuesday in April. You are told
that Aaron D. Kline, 615 North Taft, was brought to
hospital last night. Injured in fall. Skull fracture.
Died at 4:30 a.m. today. Body taken to Litton Mortuary.

You go to police department and find that Patrolman Fred
E. Denham investigated accident. You read his report
and also talk to Denham. He says Kline was painting
ceiling in kitchen of his home. Kline on stepladder.
Apparently lost his balance, fell; head struck gas
range; 10 p.m. Taken to hospital in police ambulance.
You call Roland R. Klein, county coroner. He says
inquest will not be held.

Employe of Litton Mortuary phones you. He gives you
this information about Kline:

Date and place of birth: Feb. 11, 1918, Shelby.
Parents' names: Mr. and Mrs. Fred T. Kline. Marriage,
date and place: June 14, 1940, Shelby. To whom:
Martha Elsworth of Shelby.

Occupation: Chief chemist, Humble. Joined Humble as
chemist, 1940; made chief chemist, 1952.

Education: Graduated, Shelby High school, 1936; graduated
Dexter university, 1940.

Affiliations, activities: Member, Cracc Methodist church;
Exchange club; Butler Post No. 45, American Legion.

Remarks: In Army from February, 1942, to March, 1946.

Survivors: Widow; son, Charles E., Erie; sister, Mrs.
Mary Jackson, Grossboro; brother, Harry T. Kline, Girard.

79

Funeral services, where: Grace Methodist Church. When: Thursday afternoon, 2 p.m. Minister: Rev. James G. Ballard. Burial: Roselawn Cemetery, Jonesville.

You get tied up on some other items, so it is an hour or so before you're ready to write this story. You're just finishing other work, when phone rings. It is the Star's correspondent at Salem who says he has this information for you:

Accident three miles west of Salem about an hour ago, at 9:15 a.m., on U.S. 28. Auto left highway at curve and struck tree. Driver was Mrs. Mary Jackson, Grossboro, sister of Kline. Had been told of brother's death and was on way to Jonesville. Mrs. Jackson was killed instantly, broken neck.

Information about Mrs. Jackson: Born March 3, 1926; Shelby. Graduate, Shelby High School, 1944. Married June 5, 1945, in Shelby to Homer E. Jackson of Shelby. They moved to Grossboro, 1956. Husband died 1961. Mrs. Jackson employed by Star Department Store, Grossboro, since 1961. Funeral arrangements not complete. Shelby Funeral Home in charge.

Make one story of all this, combining auto accident and fatal fall into one story.

You are the police reporter for the Sun. It's 8 p.m.
and you are checking Police Station.

Desk sergeant says auto accident at W. Rose Ave. and S.
Jefferson St. at 7 this evening. Patrolman Ralph D.
Brannon investigated. You check his report and leave
word for him to call you. A half-hour later Brannon
calls you. From his report and his phone call you have
this information:

One auto being driven north on Jefferson by Warren A.
Lacy, 46, of 514 W. Elm. Other auto driven east on
W. Rose by Paul M. Snyder, 34, 903 N. Greeley.

The two cars collided. Jefferson is the preferred street.
Snyder says he was pulling up to a stop, foot slipped
off brake pedal. Snyder's car hit left side of Lacy
car. Lacy auto swerved, jumped curb into yard, struck
tree near street.

Mrs. Lacy, 43, riding with husband. Her head struck
dash when car hit tree.

Mrs. Snyder, 32, riding in Snyder car with her husband.

Mr. and Mrs. Lacy and Mr. and Mrs. Snyder taken to Jonesville
General Hospital.

You call hospital to check on accident victims. Hospital
gives you this information:

Mr. Lacy, fractured left leg, cuts on face; condition
satisfactory. Mrs. Lacy, skull fracture; condition serious.
Mr. Snyder, fractured right arm, two broken ribs; condition
satisfactory. Mrs. Snyder, cuts and bruises on face and
left arm; released after treatment.

Write story for tomorrow morning's paper.

Suppose you are police reporter for Sun. It's 9 o'clock
on a Tuesday night in April. Sheriff's office tells you
auto accident happened at 7:30 p.m. on U.S. 28, four
miles east of Jonesville, between Jonesville and Salem.
Deputy David D. Gilmer investigated. He gives you this
information: Fred R. Sterling, 618 N. Jackson, driving
west on U.S. 28; Harold E. Johnston, Salem, driving other
auto east on U.S. 28. Rained earlier in evening. Tire
tracks indicate Sterling's car skidded on wet pavement.
His auto and Johnston's collided. Sterling's car went
into ditch; overturned.

Sterling riding alone, on way to Salem. Had telephoned
daughter, Mrs. Harold T. Wall, Salem; told her he was
coming to visit Mrs. Wall and family this evening. Mrs.
Johnston, 31, riding with Johnston. They were driving
to Jonesville. Occupants of two cars brought to
Jonesville General hospital.

You phone hospital. You are told that Sterling was
unconscious when brought to hospital. Died at 8:20;
never regained consciousness. Broken neck. Body taken
to Perry Funeral home.

Johnston has fractured left leg; condition satisfactory.
Mrs. Johnston, skull fracture, broken right arm; condition
critical. You phone Perry Funeral Home. You are given
this information about Sterling: Born; Feb. 25, 1918,
Salem. Parents; Mr. and Mrs. John B. Sterling. Married,
June 12, 1938, in Salem to Ellen Marie Pelston, Salem.
Mrs. Sterling died July 16, 1967.

Education: Graduate of Salem HS, 1936. Attended Dexter
U. two years.

Occupation: Office manager, Wilson Foundry, Inc. Took
job as bookeeper with Wilson Foundry, 1938. Became
assistant office manager, 1952; office manager, 1964.

<u>Affiliations, activities</u>: Member, Woodview Baptist church; member, Rotary club.

<u>Survivors</u>: Daughter, Mrs. Wall, Salem; son, James A. Sterling, Hobart; four grandchildren.

<u>Funeral services</u>: Thursday afternoon at 2 p.m., Woodview Baptist church. <u>Minister</u>: Rev. Alfred Foster. <u>Burial</u>: Roselawn Cemetary, Jonesville.

You phone the hospital to check again on other victims of the accident. Mrs. Johnston died at 9:15. Mr. Johnston's condition unchanged.

Body of Mrs. Johnston taken to Colton Funeral home, Salem. You phone that funeral home. You're given this information about Mrs. Johnston: Born, Aug. 20, 1938, Salem. Parents, Mr. and Mrs. Aaron E. Patterson. Graduated, Salem High School, 1956. Member of Salem Methodist Church. Survivors, parents living in Salem, and her husband. No funeral arrangements yet.

Write story for tomorrow morning's Sun.

84

You are police reporter for the morning Sun. It's early
Thursday evening in July. You are at sheriff's office
checking for news.

This morning at 8:15 accident 4 miles south of Jonesville
on U.S. 19. Converted school bus. Driving north on U.S.
19. Migrant Negro farm workers; 46 adults and children,
9 families in all. All from Waldo, Fla. Going to Michigan to work on fruit farms. To pick cherries near Hart,
Mich. For this assignment assume that Jonesville is
about halfway between Florida and Michigan.

Owner of bus, John T. Conners, 43, of Waldo driving.
Cuts and bruises; treated at Jonesville General Hospital,
then released. Deputy Vernon S. Kline investigated
accident and gives you information about it. Blowout,
Conners lost control, bus went into ditch, struck tree.
Bus badly damaged. Besides driver, 2 in bus injured:
Mrs. Homer White, 24, cuts and bruises; Frank Johnson,
10, son of Mr. and Mrs. Henry Johnson, broken left arm.
Frank and Mrs. White treated at hospital, then released.

Deputy Kline says accident happened near home of Fred C.
Whitstone, secretary of United Automobile Workers Local
843. Whitstone on way to work, stopped at accident scene,
assisted victims. Workers had very little money, no place
to go; not much clothing. Whitstone arranged for housing
at Local 843 hall, 1836 N. Marshall. Also food.

You call Whitstone. Bus repairs not to be finished until
Monday afternoon. Workers to stay at union hall until
Tuesday morning, when start on for Michigan. Whitstone
says several churches furnished food and clothing. Also
some toys for children.

You and a photographer go to union hall for several
pictures. Cots set up for workers. You talk to Conners.
He says he's been organizing labor trips for several

85

years. He's paid by farmers in Michigan. His son, Fred, helps him drive. Also several workers take turns driving. So they travel straight through; sleep while riding. Stop only for gas, rest stops and meals. Eat their meals along the road, mostly canned goods. In Michigan workers are provided with quarters similar to army barracks.

You are police reporter for the Star. Desk sergeant at
Police Station is one of your good news contacts; often
calls you when good story breaks. It's about 2 a.m. and
you are awakened by telephone ringing. It's the desk
sergeant and he tells you some of patrolmen have been
called to fire which appears to be sizable.

He says fire is at 1233 N. Clay. You drive to area
and find 1200 block of N. Clay blocked off. House at
1233 N. Clay is owned by Raymond Brannon. By the time
you get there, fire is roaring and house is almost
destroyed.

The firemen are concentrating on houses on both sides
of Brannon house. Roof of house at 1235 N. Clay had
caught on fire; wind had blown embers from Brannon
house. House at 1235 N. Clay is owned by James Callender.
Firemen are able to put out fire on roof. Firemen also
playing water on house at 1231 N. Clay; owned by Ralph
E. Cooke. Fire of Brannon house is so hot that paint
on Cooke house is beginning to blister.

Fire Chief William Kennedy is in charge of firemen. He
says fire was reported at 1:20 o'clock. You ask him about
damage. He estimates total damage at about $25,000. You
ask him what caused fire. Kennedy says it probably was
caused by defective wiring; apparently started in kitchen.
You ask him if anyone was hurt. He says Brannon girl,
Elsa, was overcome by smoke and was taken to Jonesville
General Hospital. You ask him how she got out of house,
and Kennedy says that her father, Raymond Brannon, carried
her out.

Brannon is standing nearby, so you talk to him. Brannon
says family had gone to bed several hours before; Elsa,
9 years old, and Brannon son, Charles, 13, at about 10
o'clock; Mr. and Mrs. Brannon at about 11. You ask Brannon
how he happened to wake up. He says family dog, Prince,

cocker spaniel, barked and that woke him. Prince was barking in hall. Brannon says there was a good deal of smoke in bedroom. He awakened Mrs. Brannon.

They found hall filled with smoke. Smoke was heavier in the back of house, above kitchen. Brannon says he went to children's bedrooms. He called to Charles and told him house was on fire. Charles answered and came out into hall. Elsa didn't answer. While Mrs. Brannon and Charles made their way through smoke down the stairs and to front door, Mr. Brannon went into Elsa's room. Smoke very thick in her room, which was directly above kitchen. She was unconscious. Brannon picked her up and carried her down the hall, down the stairs and into front yard.

Brannon said that by that time neighbors were awake. Mr. Callender called fire department. Brannon said that in a few minutes Elsa regained consciousness. He said she was taken in police ambulance to hospital. Mr. Brannon says that after he carried Elsa out of house, he was able to return inside and bring out small metal filing chest containing valuable papers. A few pieces of furniture were saved, but not many. You ask about insurance. Brannon says loss was covered by insurance.

Prince is at Brannon's feet. Brannon bends down and pets dog. Brannon remarks that he thinks he will buy Prince a steak. Mrs. Cooke comes out of her house, tells Brannon that Mrs. Brannon just called from hospital. She said Elsa is feeling much better.

By this time Brannon fire has died down; only a few flames seen throughout smoldering debris which fills basement. Danger to Cooke house is over; firemen quit pouring water on it.

You go back home, then a few hours later report for work at Star office. You check hospital. You are told that Elsa's condition is good; she will probably be released tomorrow. You call Fire Chief Kennedy to see if he has anything new on fire. He says that after checking it over, he estimates damage at $30,000.

Write story for today's Star.

88

You are police reporter for the morning Sun. It is about 10 on a Wednesday night in April. You hear fire sirens in downtown area. You investigate and find fire is in 200 block of S. Lafayette.

Crowd has collected; several police officers keeping people back so firemen can function effectively. Patrolmen recognize you, so you go through line to talk to Fire Chief Kennedy. You ask him where fire is, and Kennedy says it's in an apartment above Jonesville Clothing Shop. Kennedy points to man and says he's one of occupants of apartment. You talk to him; his name is Charles E. Emerson. You ask him what happened and Emerson says his wife was using cleaning fluid on some clothes in kitchen. Apparently fluid was ignited by gas stove. There was explosion and fluid was scattered throughout kitchen and into hall.

You ask if Mrs. Emerson was hurt. Emerson says no; Mrs. Emerson had just gone into living room to get sweater to clean. You ask where Emerson was and he says he was in living room watching TV. He says flames spread and there was much smoke. You ask if he or Mrs. Emerson was hurt. Emerson says no, but that their son, Fred, aged 8, was overcome by smoke. Fred was asleep in bedroom off the hall near kitchen. Emerson tried to get into bedroom, but flames stopped him.

You ask him how he was able to get to Fred. Emerson says he couldn't make it, but Mrs. Emerson had called fire department. He said firemen were there in just a few minutes. One fireman was able to get through flames and smoke and carried Fred into living room and down the stairs; had Fred wrapped in blanket, so boy was not burned. Emerson says fireman was brave; Emerson very grateful. Says Fred was taken to hospital. Mrs. Emerson has gone to hospital to be with son.

You talk to Chief Kennedy. He says fireman who carried

boy out was Russell Chappel. Both Chappel and boy were
taken to hospital. You ask if anyone else hurt; Kennedy
says no. By this time, fire has been extinguished.
Kennedy, Emerson and you go upstairs into apartment.
Kitchen badly burned; fire damage also in hallway. Also
smoke and water damage to furnishings. Kennedy estimates
damage to apartment and contents--fire, water and smoke--
at about $2,000. Emerson says loss is covered by insur-
ance.

When you go downstairs and out to sidewalk, you notice
that Howard Hall, proprieter of Jonesville Clothing Co.,
is checking through store. You ask him what damage has
been done. Hall says he's not sure yet. You tell him
you'd like to use estimate in your story. Hall agrees
to phone you at Sun office in about half an hour and
give you estimate of water and smoke damage.

You return to Sun office and phone hospital. Fred's
condition is good. He will be released tomorrow afternoon. Chappel's condition is satisfactory. Burns on
hands and face and affected by smoke. Probably will
remain in hospital 2 or 3 days.

Hall calls and tells you he estimates smoke and water
damage to merchandice and fixtures at about $6,000.
Covered by insurance.

Write story for tomorrow's Sun.

It is early in April. You are police reporter for the
Sun. It is late afternoon; you have just returned to
office after covering your beat when a windstorm begins
to develop. It increases in intensity, and you see it
is developing into important story. Rain along with
wind; some lightning.

You start checking on storm. You find number of trees
have been blown down throughout city. You talk to police
chief. He says reports indicate at least 25 trees
blown down. Some struck homes and damaged them. Also
some roofs torn off or otherwise damaged. He estimates
about 100 houses damaged.

Reports of major damage include: Roof blown off house
owned by Ronald B. Johnson, 310 N. Washington. Large
tree blown down; struck house of Clinton V. Lacey, 904
S. Lafayette; crushed front part of house. Tree blown
down in front of home of James M. Owen, 1100 E.Illinois;
wrecked station wagon owned by Owen, parked in front
of house; damaged porch of house. Wind blew off part
of roof of house owned by William D. Baker, 915 S. Marshall.

Many windows broken by wind or by flying debris. Some
large store windows blown in. Two large display windows
of Gafford's Department Store on E. Indiana broken. Two
persons cut by glass: Mrs. Clinton R. Greene, 533 E.Rose,
and Mrs. James V. Jackson, 418 Forest; had been shopping,
standing near Gafford building; trying to get some
protection from wind. Taken to Jonesville General Hospital.
Front display windows also broken at Robertson Electric
on E. Texas and Jonesville Cafe on W. Illinois.

You call hospital and are given this information: Mrs.
Greene, 43, received cut on scalp; 10 stitches needed to
close wound; condition satisfactory. Mrs. Jackson,38,
small cuts on arms and hands; treated and released.

You phone Southern Bell for statement on damage to

91

telephone service. Mr. Lindsay says falling trees broke
some telephone lines. Says about 75 phones put out of
service. All linemen working now to restore service.
Should all be repaired within couple of hours. It's 8
o'clock; Lindsay says service should be restored by 10.

You phone Mr. Edmond of Gulf States. He tells you
several power lines broken by trees, but most of them
have been repaired. Lightning struck transformer in
northeast section of city; four-block section was without electricity for half an hour. No damage to gas
lines.

You check police again. You are told that John M.
Weyerhauser,34, of 3816 Oxford taken to hospital. Works
at Humble. Coming home from work during storm. Parked
in front of house. Ran to house in rain and wind; just
then porch collapsed. Weyerhauser struck by pillar.
You call hospital. His condition serious. Has skull
fracture and broken right arm.

You phone Weather Bureau. Leslie P. Taylor says winds
reached velocity of 65 miles an hour about 5:30 p.m. An
inch of rain fell between 4 and 6 p.m. It's 10 p.m. and
wind is down to 20 miles. Taylor says forecast is for
cloudy weather tomorrow, with winds at 10 to 15 miles
per hour.

You phone Ernest D. Daniels, city street superintendant,
and ask him about damage to streets. He says some
intersections were flooded for about an hour, but that
all streets were open by 7 p.m.; no permanent damage
to streets. It's a few minutes after 10 p.m. You call
Southern Bell and Gulf States. In both cases workmen have
just completed repairs; all phone and electric service
was restored by 10 o'clock.

In the meantime another reporter has been checking for
storm damage in the county. He gives you this information:
Storm was concentrated in Jonesville area; some damage
in Salem. Warren M. Murphy, police chief of Salem, says
several trees blown down; most serious damage reported:
tree blown against house of Morton E. Caldwell; damaged
roof and porch.

The other reporter also talked to Sheriff Browne. He says

reports from farmers of several sheds blown down. Most serious damage: Barn destroyed on farm of August E. Thomson, three miles west of Jonesville on U.S. 28. Cow was killed.

Include in your story the information given you by the other reporter.

You are police reporter for the morning Sun. It's a
Tuesday afternoon in March and it's been raining heavily
since late last night. On way to office you notice
signs of flooding.

Reports indicate that parts of city are flooded--partic-
ularly northern part. Black Creek cuts through northern
edge of city; it's flooded, over its banks. Many streets
in north part of city flooded. You start checking your
news sources. You find that about one-third of area north
of Maple Blvd. and west of Wilson st. is flooded, largely
because of Black Creek; much above its banks.

By 5:30 p.m. rain has stopped, but water in Black Creek
area of city continues to rise till 7:30. It levels off,
then starts to recede at about 9. Worst area is 15-block
area bounded by Van Buren on the east, Colton on north,
Lafayette on west, and Enterprise on the south. From 2
to 3 feet of water in some of homes in that area. You
call State Police Post at Salem and find that several
roads northwest of city are under water. Bridge on
State Road 9 over Black Creek washed out, three miles
southwest of Jonesville, between Jonesville and Albion.

At about 7 p.m., you call Weather Bureau. Mr. Taylor,
forecaster, tells you that for 24-hour period ending at
6 p.m. there had been 6.4 inches of rain in Jonesville.
Forecast for next two days is cloudy and mild.

Then you call Police Station again. Desk sergeant says
body of missing boy found in flooded area of city. Name:
Gordon T. Butler, 14, son of Mr. and Mrs. Thomas G. Butler,
1221 N. Lafayette. Had been missing since 5 p.m. Gordon,
freshman at Central HS, phoned home at 3:30 today; told
mother would not be home until about 4:30; wanted to stop
at friend's house on way home. Friend: Bernard Quinn,14,
son of Mr. and Mrs. Russell W. Quinn, 904 N. Jefferson.
Gordon still not home at 5. Mrs. Butler called Quinn
residence; Gordon had left for home at about 4:15.

95

Mrs. Butler called husband at his store; he phoned
police, reporting son was missing. Search started by
police. Body found at about 6:15 p.m. in deep ditch
along street in 1100 block of N. Jefferson. Boy had
been dead about two hours. Apparently walking home
during heavy rain. Rain then so heavy, a downpour;
boy apparently became confused; walked into deep ditch,
drowned; could not swim. Patrolman Ralph E. Brannon
found body in ditch.

Body is at Perry Funeral Home. You call Perry's. Funeral
arrangements not yet made. Gordon, member of Grace
Methodist Church. Surviving: parents; sister, Mary,
at home; grandparents, Mr. and Mrs. Carl Butler, Shelby,
and Mrs. Homer Harkness, Salem.

At about 9:30 you call Ernest D. Daniels, city street
superintendent. He says water has started to receed.
Northwest section, lowest part of city, still flooded,
but not appear that city streets are badly damaged. He
believes normal travel resumed through northwest area of
city in two days.

Write story for tomorrow's Sun.

It's a Wednesday night in February. You are city hall
reporter for morning Sun. City council is meeting tonight;
you are covering it to write story for tomorrow's Sun.
Mayor Alvin C. Baker presides; meeting is in City Hall.

Warren H. Richardson, 806 East Poplar ave., attends
meeting. Requests rezoning of 800 block of E. Poplar
from residential to commercial. Says he owns three
adjacent lots on block. Wants to build and operate
grocery store. Council refers Richardson to City
Zoning board.

Paving of two blocks of East Rose ave. is discussed.
They are 1800 and 1900 blocks. Councilman Norman J.
Decker says petition was presented month ago asking
that the two blocks of street be paved. He said only
two residents of street attended council meeting and
protested. Council orders street to be paved; cost to
be assessed to owners of property along street.

Councilman Arthur N. Harper says it is time they do
something about downtown traffic. He says some streets
should be designed for one-way traffic. He says streets
in center of business district should be alternated, one
go east, the next west; others, one street go north, and
next south, etc. He says these streets probably by
involved: Van Buren, Marshall, Jefferson, Lafayette,
Wilson, Clay, Michigan, Illinois, Indiana, and Kentucky
streets.

Councilman Ernest R. Payne says he agrees. Other cities
use system and it helps eliminate traffic jams; he says
traffic can move faster. Councilman Albert T. Hall says
some merchants are for such a plan, some against, but
he thinks it would be good idea. After some discussion
Mayor Baker appoints Harper and Payne as committee, Harper
as chairman. They're to confer with City Engineer Patrick
N. Faris, Police Chief Alvin E. Jackson, and Fire Chief

William N. Kennedy, then draft plan; present it at March 20 meeting of council. Then public hearing on proposed ordinance could be held in April.

Arthur D. Bailey, city manager, says city ought to buy another heavy-duty street sweeper. He says city has grown too large for the one sweeper. Ernest D. Daniels, street superintendent, is at meeting. Bailey asks him about street sweeping schedule. Daniels says his men can't do too good a job with one sweeper. Mayor Baker tells Bailey to check into cost of new sweeper and report at next council meeting.

Requests for liquor and beer permits are presented by city clerk. Requests are for Mike's Bar, 3210 East Kentucky st., Connie's Club, 1806 South Van Buren St. and Lou's Lounge, 2401 North Jefferson St. Public hearing is set for March 20 meeting.

Councilman Alfred A. Oden says we should get started on a program of increasing recreation facilities. He says the three baseball diamonds in City Park can't handle demand when Little League starts for summer. He says last year more teams were in program than ever before. He says it looks as though there will be even more this year. Not enough room for more diamonds in City Park, but he thinks there's an answer. City Park is in south-central part of Jonesville. City owns some property in north part of city, in 1700 block of North Marshall st. Room for two baseball diamonds.

Oden also says tennis courts in City Park have become very crowded. Six courts. Says 2 more should be built; there's room. Also on Marshall street property four tennis courts could be built. Other councilmen agree that recreation facilities should be expanded. Mayor authorizes City Engineer to draw up plans and estimate costs for baseball diamonds and tennis courts and report at March 20 meeting.

It is during the second week of March and you are cover-
ing night meeting of City Council for tomorrow's Star.
Mayor Baker presides at meeting. Action is taken by
Council on following issues in this order:

Petition is received from residents of 2800 block of
North Clay street for sidewalks to be constructed.

Councilman Albert E. Hall says something should be done
about driving in City Park. Says it is dangerous for
children playing in park. Speed limit 30 miles an hour.
Too fast, Hall says. He moves it be cut to 20. Seconded.
Motion passes.

Ernest D. Daniels, street superintendent, is at meeting.
Tells council one of city's street maintainance trucks
broke down this week. He says estimates from garages,
would cost over $550 to recondition. Says not worth
repairing. Councilman Fred E. Fitch moves bids be
accepted for 5-ton truck. Seconded. Motion passes.
Bids to be opened April 13.

Father Thomas H. Murphy of St. Joseph Catholic church and
Reverend Alfred Foster, pastor of Woodview Baptist church
are at meeting. Murphy says he and Foster want to present petition signed by all pastors of city. Petition
asks that positive action be taken by Council to curb
juvenile delinquency. In petition are such examples as
thefts by teen-agers, drinking at student parties, and
vandalism. Suggested in petition: set up juvenile
delinquency commission of council members and private
citizens. Murphy and Foster both speak in favor of
idea. Councilman Norman A. Decker says annual police
report shows substantial increase in juvenile delinquency
in past year. Mayor Baker appoints Decker and Payne to
be committee to study matter. Committee to make recommendation as to commission idea at April 27 meeting of
Council.

99

Amendment to city building code introduced for May 11
public hearing. Would require barrier type curbs for
all parking facilities adjacent to street right of way.
Would prevent entering or leaving lots except at en-
trances and exits provided. Curbs must be set back so
that cars will not extend over sidewalk. Curbs must
be at least 6 inches high.

Proposed amendment to beer and liquor ordinance is discussed. Public hearing on amendment set for May 11.
City treasurer Glen E. Nash appears before council. Says
present ordinance allows bartender to begin work without
license; requires him to apply for license within 15
days. Enforcement officers find many bartenders claiming they have just started on job. Amendment would
require bartenders to apply before beginning to work;
bartender would be given temporary permit to be used
until regular license is issued.

Proposal to four-lane N. Jefferson St. from Maple Blvd.
to Mason St. is discussed. A city engineer's report on
proposal is read. Still working on cost estimates.
Council authorizes Mayor Baker to discuss with State
Highway dept. officials to determine if project could
be done by state. Under proposed arrangement, city would
repay cost in installments over period of several years.
Baker will open negotiations with state next week.

Council orders installation of new sewers in the 2200
block of N. Wilson st., 1800 block of E. Tulip av. and
600 block of Oxford street.

City engineer Patrick N. Farris appears before Council.
He says he needs another assistant, to bring number up
to four. He says staff is same size as 10 years ago,
but amount of work handled by his office is much greater.
Area of city has increased 30 per cent through annexa-
tion during 10-year period. Council approves hiring
another assistant at not more than $900 a month.

It is the second week of April and you are covering
night meeting of City Council for tomorrow morning's
Sun. Mayor Alvin E. Baker presides. Action taken by
Council on following items in this order:

Application is read for liquor and beer permit for Star-
light Lounge, 1824 North Wilson. Moved and seconded
that application be approved. Motion passes.

William H. Preston appears before Council. Says he is
owner of property at 730-38 West Oak. Says he had asked
City Zoning Board to rezone the 700 block of West Oak
from residential to commercial. Says Zoning Board had
rejected his request at March meeting. Now he is appealing decision of Zoning Board.

Preston says he wants to build store building; would
lease it to grocery chain. Says store building would
be of attractive design, brick and steel construction;
off-street parking lot at rear of building. John C.
Princeton, 723 West Oak, speaks against rezoning. Presents petition signed by 22 property owners of 700 and
800 blocks of West Oak, opposing rezoning. It is moved
and seconded that Council reject Preston's appeal.
Motion passes, so Preston's appeal is rejected.

Councilman Albert T. Hall says he has been working with
city health officer, Dr. Henry F. Mayes, on an amendment
to city health code. Dr. Mayes is attending Council
meeting. Hall says amendment would require all food
handlers to have health card. X-ray examination for
tuberculosis and other medical tests would be required
before card is issued.

Dr. Mayes takes floor and explains some provisions of proposed amendment. Term "food handler"--anyone working
where food in any form is offered to public. Such as
waitresses and cooks in restaurants, soda fountain

clerks, clerks in grocery stores. Dr. Mayes says he's
studied ordinances of other cities and proposed amendment is similar; says it should be adopted. Says many
business establishments would be effected. Council
votes to hold public hearing on proposed amendment at
Council meeting May 10.

Councilman Alfred A. Oden says something should be done
about drainage problem in northern part of city. Whenever
heavy rain, large area floods. Councilman Hall agrees;
many residents complaining. Situation dangerous. Reminds
council that boy drowned last month (Gordon T. Butler, 14,
son of Mr. and Mrs. Thomas G. Butler, 1221 N. Lafayette
St. according to clipping from newspaper's library).
Other councilmen agree action should be taken. Mayor Baker
tells City Manager Arthur E. Bailey to begin a study of
problem.

Councilman Norman J. Decker introduces amendment to city
traffic code. Clinton V. Lacy, city attorney, explains
it. Lacy says there have been a number of accidents on
parking lots of shopping centers and supermarkets, but
present city code not adequate. Police can't file
proper charges. Amendment would make it traffic vio-
lation to drive while intoxicated on parking lot. Public
hearing set for May 10 Council meeting.

Councilman Arthur M. Harper says he's been interested in
improving city recreation facilities. He says he's
written to a number of cities in Jonesville population
range about problem. He thinks city park on N. Clay
street should be made into more of a family recreation
center. He says picnic tables and softball diamonds are
all right, but there should be more recreation facilities.

Harper thinks there should also be swimming pool, wading
pool, tennis courts, skating rink and archery range.
Several councilmen comment and agree it would be good,
but wonder about cost. Mayor appoints Councilmen Harper,
Fred E. Fitch and Ernest R. Paine as committee to study
matter, Harper as chairman. Committee to make report at
May 10 meeting. To give cost estimates and recommend
which facilities should be built for this year and which
should be added next year.

102

It is early in March. You are covering tonight's monthly
meeting of Jonesville Board of Education for tomorrow
morning's Sun. Meeting is held in superintendent's office
in Central High School. All members present: Decker,
president of board, who presides; Cooke, Butler, Gardner,
O'Brien. Also attending: Superintendent Rayborn, Paul
T. Sanford, principal of Central high school; Russell W.
Oatis, president of Jonesville Teachers association.

Rayborn reports that Lampton Elementary School needs
new roof. Says it should be done this summer. Leaks
reported in three rooms; damage to walls, furniture and
supplies. Board members discuss matter; agree it should
be done. Motion that bids be opened at May 9 meeting;
work to be done in June. Seconded; motion carried.

Rayborn says he needs another stenographer for his office.
Board discusses matter. Moved, seconded that Rayborn be
authorized to hire another stenographer. Motion carried.

Butler, chairman of salary committee, says he wants to
bring up teachers' salary question. Says he and the
other committee members, Cook and O'Brien, have met three
times studying matter. Once officers of Jonesville
Teachers Association met with committee. Butler says
committee recommends 5 per cent increase for all teachers
in city school system. Total increase of about $93,000
for 310 teachers; average annual increase of about $300.

Oatis speaks in favor of raise. Says two years since
general salary increase. Says present pay scale is 4
per cent higher than five years ago; cost of living 10
per cent higher than 5 years ago.

Board members discuss matter. Moved and seconded that
teachers be given 5 per cent raise starting in September.
Motion carried.

103

Rayborn says sidewalks should be replaced at Central high school and Tanner Elementary school this summer. Moved that bids be opened at April 11 meeting. Motion carried.

Applications for two sabbatical leaves are read. Leaves for next school year at half pay asked by Miss Juanita A. Edwards and Glenn D. Stephens. Miss Edwards plans to take graduate work at Columbia University. Mr. Stephens plans to take graduate work at University of Pennsylvania. Miss Edwards member of Central High School 9 years; Mr. Stephens, 11 years at Central HS. Board grants leaves.

This is a Thursday night in April. Board of Education
is holding monthly meeting at Central High School.
Thomas E. Decker, president of Board presides. You are
covering meeting to write story for tomorrow's Sun.

Bids are opened for tables for Central High School lunch
room. Bids were: Gafford's Department store, $734.12;
Caldwell Hardware & Paint Co., $682.40; Princeton Furni-
ture Co., $741.20. Caldwell bid accepted.

Resignation of Phillip R. Adams, Central High School
teacher is read. Reason given: ill health. Adams is
63. Regular retirement age to qualify for pension is
65. School physician recommends that his resignation
be accepted; also recommends Adams be granted state
pension. Board accepts resignation, effective June 1.
Also passes resolution, addressed to State Board of
Education, recommending Adams be granted full pension.
Passes another resolution, commending Adams for long
service to school.

City Recreation department submits request in writing;
asks use of Central High school gymnasium for Friday
nights during summer. Plans to hold dances for teen-
agers. Asks use of gym free of charge. Several board
members say it's good thing; may help hold down juvenile
delinquency. Board votes on request. Request is
granted.

Board opens bids on addition and remodeling project at
Central High school. Bids are: Franklin Construction
Co., Erie, $77,120; Nelson & Miller Contractors, Jones-
ville, $73,275; Ralph T. Paulson Co., Warren, $75,210.
Contract is awarded to Nelson & Miller on their low
bid.

Three-room addition: new chemistry laboratory, chemistry stock room, and 75-seat classroom. Old chemistry

laboratory adjacent to biology laboratory. Contract calls for remodeling work: knock out partition, make two rooms into one big room, to be enlarged biology laboratory. Work on addition and remodeling to start between June 1 and 10. Work to be completed by Sept. 1; ready for use next fall.

Robert N. Rayborn, superintendent of schools is at meeting. He says repairs should be made to Bradford Elementary School roof. It leaks. A number of books in school library damaged during heavy rain last week. Also desks and other equipment in two classrooms. Thomas G. Butler, member of board, asks how old is roof. Rayborn says over 25 years. Butler says roof should be replaced, not repaired. Other board members agree. Moved to accept bids for new roof at May 21 meeting. Motion is carried.

After meeting you ask Rayborn about Adams. He checks his records and gives you this additional information about Adams: Native of Gilead; graduate of Gilead HS. Graduate of Dexter University. Taught at Bradley High school for 6 years, then returned to Dexter. Received M.A. degree. Then joined Central HS faculty at Jonesville 32 years ago. Has taught English since that time. Married, lives at 932 East Tennessee st. Has son, Charles T. Adams, living in Morton.

You are a reporter for the Sun. The Sun's regular correspondent at Ottawa is ill, and there is an important
meeting of Ottawa Board of education tonight. Its
regular January meeting. In view of correspondent's
sickness, you are sent to Ottawa to cover board meeting.

As usual it's held in high school. Various items considered. One matter is very important, and you will
make separate story of it. In this story no reference
will be made to other items transacted by board.

This is item in question. At September meeting a proposal was brought up. It was the possibility of
establishing evening college. It was argued pro and
con at that time. Fred R. Smith, President of Board
appointed committee to study matter and to report on it.
Committee: Frank T. Johnson, Chairman; Elbert S. Sample
and Wilbur D. Hooker. (All members of board, of course.)

At tonight's meeting Mr. Johnson says he's ready to
report. He and other two committee members have looked
into matter thoroughly. They first contacted State
Department of Public Instruction. Director of department said evening college could be established. He
said there would be certain requirements to be met.
Such things as staff and physical facilities.

The director, Moran T. Sites, said he and his dept. would
cooperate. He said full-time dean to be in charge would
be needed. Also three other full-time faculty members;
also enough instructors with advanced degrees who could
teach part-time. Sites wanted to know where classes
would be held. Committee said, in classrooms of Ottawa
High School in evenings, when they were not being used
by high school students. Sites said that would be all
right.

Johnson said committee talked to Dr. Elton E. Tower,

president of State University at Grossboro; also Dr. James A. Gardiner, president of Dexter U. Both said they would cooperate.

Johnson said library problem could be solved. High school library could be made available to evening college students. Sites outlined library requirements. Johnson said about 500 books would need to be added to bring library up to minimum requirements.

Johnson said committee proposed that enough basic courses be offered so student could get first year's work of regular college course. Tower and Gardiner told committee that if curriculum approved by State Dept. of Public instruction, student could take 30 semester hours in evening college and then enter State Univ. or Dexter as sophomore.

Johnson said that the committee made a survey of local public school teachers. He said there were a number of teachers with advanced degrees and sufficient experience; so no problem of finding part-time instructors. He said about 20 said they would apply; probably 5 or 6 would be hired first year.

Johnson also talked about courses to be given. He said curriculum hadn't been mapped out definitely. But courses would include history, English, government, sociology, at least one science and at least one foreign language.

Board discussed committee's report. Board voted to go ahead with project. Smith told committee to start taking applications for dean of evening college. Johnson said they would do that and report again. Smith said he thought board should appoint a dean April 1 so the dean could make plans to start instruction next September.

Board agreed they wanted college to begin in September. Smith said dean could help select instructors. Instructors probably would be hired by July 1. Board voted that the committee go ahead with taking applications for dean; also to order necessary books for library.

Assume it is early in April. You are city hall reporter
for the afternoon Star. You are making your rounds this
morning in city hall and are talking to Mayor Baker.
Baker says he has a story for you. He says he finally
has announcement on new position of Director of Recreation. City Council has been considering matter for
several months. Baker says Joseph R. Quall has been
appointed.

Quall is teacher and assistant football coach at Central
High School here. Baker says Quall will take over his
new job June 15. He's resigned at school, but will finish
out semester. He's been assistant football coach and
teacher at Central High School since 1964.

You ask Baker what the new job covers. He says Quall will
supervise all city recreation facilities. Mayor Baker
says City council has been planning to expand whole city
recreation program. Quall will be in charge of building
up program. City playgrounds, recreation center, tennis
courts and softball diamonds will be under his supervision. His salary will be $10,800. Present time,
Arthur D. Bailey, City manager, has general supervision
of recreation program, along with other duties. But
expanded program, full-time director needed, Mayor says.

Then you phone Quall to get background information about
him. He says he graduated from Central High school in
1958. Other data: At Central, member of football team
for three years and also took part in school dramatics;
attended Dexter from September, 1958, to June, 1962;
received bachelor's degree, June, 1962; majored in physical education; was tackle on Dexter football team for
three years. Served in Army 1962-64.

You ask Quall if he has started making plans about his
new job. He answers yes; says he has several things in
mind in new activities for recreation program. He's

109

going to enlarge supervised program for youngsters. But
Quall says he has plans for all ages. More activities
for adults, such as art, modeling, hobby classes, square
dance classes. Quall says recreation personnel will be
increased to carry out this expanded program. Plans
to hire some Dexter university students, part-time.
Quall hopes to make recreation program more of a year-
round program; to build up winter activities.

Then you phone Robert N. Raybourn, superintendent of
schools. You ask him if someone has been hired to take
Quall's place at Central. He says no one hired yet;
expects to hire new teacher and assistant football coach
for next fall by July 1.

50 / ROCKS CONTROVERSY

You're city hall reporter for the Star. You are making
rounds on a Tuesday morning, contacting various news
sources. City clerk tells you Councilman Albert T. Hall
might have story about rocks along streets. You contact Hall. He is chairman of City Council's Public
Works committee. He says, yes, he certainly does have
story about rocks. He's been having plenty of trouble
with rocks.

You ask him what he means, and he says, rocks along
rights of way of city streets. You ask him, What kind
of trouble? So he explains.

Rights of way for most city streets extend each side of
paved or gravelled portion 6 to 10 feet. This 6- to
10-foot strip is between actual street and citizens'
property. Many cases, 6 to 10 feet forms part of lawn
of property next to it. Nice grass, etc. Property
owners mow it, etc. City lets them use it as part of
their lawn.

You say, that's nice, but where's the trouble? Hall says
people don't want lawns cut up by autos running over it.
So they haul in rocks and line their yards. What's wrong
with that? you ask. Hall says there's a city ordnance
against rocks on street rights of way like that. You
ask him why. And he says, possible damage to autos.

Hall says ordnance not very popular; city hasn't enforced
it. But recently several cars damaged when they hit the
rocks. For instance, one car, nothing but a flat tire,
but driver lost control; hit a large rock on right of way.
$500 damage, front end of car. Other cases, serious
damage to cars. Car owners and insurance companies complaining about rocks, says Hall.

So a month ago Council discussed matter, then authorized
Ernest E. Daniels, street superintendent, to have his

111

men notify people to move rocks back to property line.
Deadline set for last Wednesday. Property owners
started complaining in great numbers, and heatedly.
Complained to Daniels, to Hall, to mayor, other councilmen, city clerk. Such a time, says Hall. Both
sides--car owners and insurance companies on one, and
home owners on the other--have a good argument, says
Hall.

So Hall made a study of situation. He toured city.
Main trouble, some of rocks very big--also right near
the pavement. Some of the rocks are so large they would
easily wreck a car, Hall says. Some of them foot and a
half high. So Hall is going to offer plan at Council
meeting Thursday night of this week. Sort of compromise.

Hall says it will be as an amendment to ordnance. If
amendment is passed, it would be all right to have rocks
along the street if not closer than 3 feet to pavement
or graveled part, and if rocks are not more than 6
inches high. That way, Hall says, maybe no one will complain too much. Property owners can keep and protect
most of their lawns; rocks will discourage driving onto
lawn; but rocks won't be big enough to wreck cars. And
he says he will insist there is strict enforcement of
ordnance as amended.

Write story for today's Star.

112

You are a reporter for the morning Sun. You are schools
reporter and are at Central High school this afternoon.
It is early in May. You check Mr. Rayborn, superintendent of schools. He says he's ready to announce a good
story.

He refers to action taken by Board of Education last
month. Board voted to create new position at Central
high. New position: dean of students. Board has been
considering matter several months. Rayborn conducted
study; made report at last month's board meeting. Action
on this matter was one of number of items of business
transacted by Board and included in story of board meeting, carried in Sun the next day. Reference to new position was rather brief, as details had not been worked
out. Board at that time authorized Rayborn to appoint
dean from Central faculty.

Now Mr. Rayborn says he's ready to announce that Harry B.
Emerson has been appointed. Emerson is an English teacher
at Central. Rayborn refers to personnel records and gives
you this information about Emerson: Native of Jonesville.
Graduated, Central HS, 1948; bachelor's degree in education with honors, Dexter, 1952; activities at Dexter,
member of University Band, debate team, dramatics; teacher,
Erie High School, 1952-55; master's degree in education,
Dexter, 1956; hired as English teacher, Central high.
faculty, 1956. Coach of debate team, 1962 to present.

Rayborn says main job of dean of students: curriculum
planning for students. Faculty members who are student
advisers to be supervised by dean. Dean also to coor-
dinate school activities, such as dramatics, publica-
tions, music groups and honor societies.

Rayborn tells you to see Emerson and have him fill you
in on details of plans mapped out. Emerson says his
office will be primarily interested in seeing individual

113

students have appropriate curricula. He says all pupils
in grades 8 through 11 will be given aptitude tests
this month. About July 15, his office to mail results
of tests to parents. Envelope to include return post
card; parents to state whether college training for
student is probable, or improbable.

Aptitude tests, probability of college training, student preference learned from interviews: all to help
determine appropriate courses for each student for next
September. If college unlikely, more emphasis on voca-
tional subjects. Try to see each student taking best
curriculum for him.

A continuing program. Each year, eighth graders take
tests and report sent to parents, with return card enclosed.
Also, each year, grades 9 through 11, parents will be asked
to report if there is change in college probability. If
change, adjust curriculum accordingly.

As to coordination of activities. Student advisers to
keep close watch on individual's activities. Amount of
participation to depend upon grades. Not let any students
be overburdened with activities to extent that grades
suffer.

Write story for tomorrow morning's paper.

You are schools reporter for the Star. It is a Wednesday morning early in December and you are covering your beat for today's Star. Robert N. Rayborn, supt. of schools, tells you he can now announce merit pay story. You knew this story had been developing for some time, but you didn't know details.

Rayborn says that for several years he's felt there should be merit pay system for teachers. Principal of high school and other school officials have agreed. Last spring Rayborn brought subject up at a Board of Education meeting. Board authorized him to make study of it and present such plan. Board said that it would favor a fund in budget to finance it.

In September Rayborn appointed teachers' committee; Anthony J. Vance of Central High School, chairman. They met several times. Also wrote to schools having such a plan and got information from them. Committee made preliminary draft. Then met with Rayborn, Paul E. Sandford, high school principal, and Miss Linda A. Norwood of Lampton Elementary school, representing the elementary school principals. They all studied project at two meetings and made a few revisions.

Now, Rayborn says, he and Sandford will study it further. Not to make changes, but to arrive at cost estimates. Then Rayborn will present it to school board at board meeting in January.

You ask Rayborn how system would work. He says point system will be used. A maximum of 100 points. Score of 80 would be minimum. This is, a teacher would need 80 or more to be qualified to receive merit recognition. That would mean extra pay over regular scale, if teacher's application is acted on favorably.

The 100 points awarded in various catagories; catagories

115

to carry these maximums: general atmosphere of classroom, 8; teacher preparation, 20; classroom management, 24; presentation, 32; personal qualities, 16. You ask more about total of 100 points. Rayborn says there are sub- topics under the catagories, a total of 25 subtopics. Each subtopic worth a maximum of 4 points. He says scoring on subtopics: 4 points for rating of "superior"; Catagory of general atmosphere of classroom has 2 sub- topics, teacher preparation has 5, classroom 6, presen- tation 8, personal qualities 4.

You ask, What about these subtopics? Rayborn gives you several examples.

One is: Teacher has attractive, informative, and appro- priate materials on display to stimulate learning.

Another: Teacher understands subject matter well and indicates interest in broadening his fund of knowledge.

Another: Teacher plans activities to meet individual needs and differences for slow, average, and gifted learners.

You ask how this will be done. Rayborn says there will be an evaluation committee to process each application. He says it will inciude 3 teachers, plus superintendent or his representative, and a principal. Teachers for committees will be drawn from a pool. He says for each application there will be classroom visits and a conference of teacher and committee.

You ask if any teacher would be eligible to apply. Ray- born says that they need to have at least a bachelor's degree and have taught in Jonesville school system at least 3 years.

He says systems similar to this one have worked out well in a number of cities throughout nation.

Rayborn says if plan is adopted, a score of 80 won't auto- matically guarantee merit raise. It will depend on amount of money available. Also, all merit raises not necessarily for same amount; it will depend upon score made by teacher.

53 / RETIREMENT PLAN

You are a reporter for the morning Sun. It is a Wednesday
evening in January and you are attending meeting of board
of trustees of Dexter University in Harris Hall.

Alfred D. Gaines, Jonesville, president of board, presides.
Several items of business are transacted. You decide to
write separate story on this one item. (In this story
you make no reference to other items of business.) This
is item in question:

Dr. James A. Gardiner, president of the university,
reports on a study for a proposed retirement plan for
faculty and staff members of the university. Gardiner
says study was made by a committee appointed four
months ago and headed by Dr. Robert F. Wilson, comptroller
of the university. Other members were Dr. Philip F.
MacDonald, Dean of Graduate School, and Dr. Clinton R.
Greene of Geography Department. Dr. Gardiner says he
approves of committee's recommendations.

Committee recommends retirement plan, 25 to 50% of
salary. Rate would depend upon how long person had
paid into plan. Retirement pay to start at age 65. To
finance plan, employe would contribute 4% of pay through
payrole deduction, university would contribute 8%.
Retirement pay would be 25 to 50% of average for last
5 years full-time pay at university. 10 years service
at university as minimum to be eligible to draw retirement pay.

Gardiner says retirement plan needed to reduce turnover
of faculty. Present plan, a change-of-work status, does
not offer enough. Now at age 65, employe is given reduced
working load; pay is cut in half; can work until 70, then
removed from payrole.

Committee study included report on 10 institutions of
about same size as Dexter, but having retirement plan.
117

All 10 more successful than Dexter at holding faculty
members; turnover rate for all ranged from 20 to 40%
below Dexter figure.

Committee report shows proposed plan would cost university
about $150,000 a year. Board votes to adopt retirement
plan, to start with persons retiring in June of this year.
Also, plan will be made retroactive for faculty and
staff members already retired on change of work status
and having minimum of 10 years of full-time service.
They will not contribute to plan, so will receive from
10 to 25% of regular salary.

You are a reporter for the Sun. Your beat includes
Dexter University. You are making rounds at university
on a Wednesday early in October and you call on Dr.
Philip F. McDonald, Dean of Graduate School.

McDonald says he believes he has story for you. He
says a graduate student is studying at Dexter as a
Woodrow Wilson fellow. You ask if that is something
special, and McDonald says yes, it's a fine program.
You ask McDonald questions about this type of fellowship.

You ask McDonald, Who sponsors the fellowships? He
replies, the Woodrow Wilson National Fellowship Foundation. He says program is financed by Ford Foundation. You ask McDonald other questions. One question:
Does the program have a special purpose? Yes, it's to
aid graduate students who plan to go into college
teaching. How much do the fellowships pay? McDonald
says, $1,500 cash, plus tuition and allowance for
dependents.

You ask McDonald the name of student who is studying
at Dexter as a Woodrow Wilson fellow. McDonald says it's
Arthur C. Daniel of Byron. His parents are Mr. and Mrs.
Charles T. Daniel of Byron. He graduated from Byron
High school, then from Grossboro College last June.·
Majored in French. Graduated from Grossboro with honors.
Member of Phi Kappa Phi, national scholastic honor society.
Working toward Master of Arts degree in foreign languages.
Enrolled at the start of the fall semester. He is not
married.

McDonald says fellowship foundation grants 1,000 fellowships each year. Several Dexter graduates have been
awarded scholarships in past few years for graduate study
at other institutions. But this is first person to study
at Dexter under the program. Ones who receive fellowships

119

may choose any accredited graduate school in U.S. or
Canada except where they got their undergraduate training.

McDonald says Daniel rooms at 1121 W. Illinois and he
gives you his phone number. You return to Sun office
and call Daniel. You verify facts and spelling of names,
then question him further.

You ask him why he decided to choose teaching foreign
language as a career. Daniel says his high school
mathematics teacher should get the credit. You ask
him to explain. Daniel says when he was sophomore in
high school, he was having trouble with algebra.
Became very discouraged; about decided to quit school
as soon as he became 16. But finally talked to
mathematics instructor. Math teacher was patient with
him, got him straightened out so he was able to pass
algebra. Instructor urged him to finish high school.
Also said Daniel should go to college. Math teacher
told him he'd better take a foreign language, if he
planned to go to college. Daniel enrolled for French
course; found he enjoyed it very much and seemed to
have talent for foreign language. That's why he
decided to major in French at Grossboro College and
finally decided to go into college teaching.

You ask Daniel why he chose Dexter for graduate work.
Daniel says, well, for one thing it's not far from
home. Also, his math instructor got his B.A degree
from Grossboro and his master's at Dexter. You ask
Daniel what the high school math teacher's name is.
Daniel says it's Robert E. Gordon. Daniel says he's
still teaching at Byron HS, and he's still a close friend
of Daniel.

Write story for tomorrow's Sun.

You are a reporter for the Sun. This evening you are
covering January meeting of Men's club of First
Presbyterian church. Meeting is in church parlors.
75 members present. Speaker is Vice Mayor Fred C.
Fitch. Arthur M. Harper presides. He's president
of club. He introduces Fitch. Write story for
tomorrow morning's paper.

The text of Fitch's speech follows:

I'm glad to have the opportunity to speak to you
gentlemen tonight. In fact, I'm sure I represent
all members of the City Council in commending you
for your interest in your local government. More
citizens should be interested. Their tax money is
financing this extensive operation for their benefit.
And, to be sure, it is an extensive operation.
For example, the Public Works Department alone
employs 128 people. And the department engages in
many activities and performs a great variety of
services.
The department's Engineering division last year
reviewed and approved eight subdivisions complying
with city regulations. The inspection division last
year issued building permits valued at more than $10
million. The division's personnel also made 8,000
building, plumbing and electrical inspections.
Impressive figures can also be given in relation to
other departments.
Consider the Fire Department. The firemen not only
put out fires; they work hard at preventing them. Last
year the fire prevention bureau inspected 8,500 homes
and 900 business establishments for fire hazards. This
effort has not been in vain. Jonesville's fire insurance
rates are cheaper than those of any other sizable city
in the state.
Another very important activity of local government,
of course, pertains to public school education. More

121

than 300 teachers are employed in the Jonesville schools.
The pupils number 7,300.

Public works--fire protection--public education.
These are only three of the many phases of local
government. And of course, they are the most generally
known activities of local government. Ones which
you perhaps think of first when local government is
mentioned.

What about some of the other services which you are
receiving? They come from a number of departments.
You may know that the departments exist, but very
likely you are not aware of the scope of their
activities.

I'm sure that you all are aware of the City Health
Unit, but are you familiar with the size of the
department and the scope of its operations? How
large a staff does it have? Three employes? Six?
The Health Unit has twelve full-time employes. Do
you really understand what the Health unit does?

Its public health nursing program includes an
immunization program, offering polio and smallpox
vaccines, and injections for diptheria, whooping
cough and tetanus. The public health nurse cooperates
with the School Board in planning health programs for
children.

The Health unit also conducts maternal, dental,
venereal disease and welfare clinics.

The unit gives home nursing instructions to families
having a chronic-disease patient, suffering from heart
disease, diabetes, cancer and other diseases.

The communicable disease program of the unit concen-
trates on an intensive case-finding tuberculosis program.

The unit's sanitation program supervises about 250
food-handling establishments: bars, cold storage and
locker plants, poultry and slaughter sheds. The Health
Unit's program also extends to milk inspection and pest
control.

It's easy to see that the Health Unit is an important
department of local government.

You men are all familiar with the City Library. You
probably have visited it many times. But did you every
stop to consider the size of that operation? Last year
the library lent over 110,000 books, a 14 per cent increase
in lending over the previous year. Four thousand reference
questions were answered last year.

The work of many other departments could be cited,

122

but I think these are representative enough to point out the variety and scope of activities included in our local government.

These are your activities. You are footing the bill. Also you are benefiting from them. So once again, I commend you for displaying an interest in your local government. Also, I urge that you retain and develop that interest.

Attend Council and other public meetings. Follow carefully all governmental activities as reported in newspaper stories. Learn as much about your local government as you can.

As a taxpayer, you should see that you're getting your money's worth. As a citizen, you should see that the community is getting the best government possible.

It's April and quarterly meeting of State Retail Food
Dealers Association is being held tonight in the Jonesville
Hotel. You're covering it for tomorrow's Sun. 200
present. Martin B. Hughes of Grossboro, president of
association, presides.

Speaker is Fred T. Johnson of Columbus, Ohio, president
of National Association of Retail Grocers. In your
story on speech include pertinent facts and figures.
Text of speech follows:

This is my first trip to your state, and I want to
say that I envy you fellows. This is truly a sports-
man's paradise. I came here from Columbus by plane
today, and I had a chance to see the wonderful fishing
and hunting areas here. This is my first trip, but
definitely not my last. Before the year is over, I
intend to return for a fishing vacation.

But enough of that. You're not interested in my
vacation plans. Let's forget the bass and blue gills
and get down to a little serious business.

Let's look at some of the problems confronting the
food dealers. There's no question--they've really
multiplied during recent years. There have been many
changes.

My grandfather operated a small country town grocery.
I recall spending many an hour in that little store when
I was a small boy. It seemed like the center of much
activity then--and of course it was, for relatively its
place was among the leaders for hustle and bustle.

Now, as I look back, I'm amazed by the simplicity of
the operation. Mr grandfather's customers were stable.
He rarely lost one unless the family moved away. We
had two grocery stores in our town, so my grandfather
had roughly one half of the householders as his
customers.

Maintaining the stock of goods was comparatively
simple. Many of the items were in bulk--and usually

125

all you needed in such a case was a selection of one.
Even in canned goods, the customer was satisfied with
a choice of perhaps two brands and/or grades.

Then gradually brands, grades and types of foods
increased. The inventory of the average grocery
store kept going forward in amount. More and more
initial investment was needed to start a business.
More and more money was needed to keep a grocery at
a stock level acceptable to the customer. The small
grocery store began to come closer and closer to big
business year by year. And as the operation grew
larger it also became more complicated and speculative.

During the past few years labor costs have been rising.
Food production costs and overhead have gone up,
whittling away at what is needed for a satisfactory
profit. Just what are the prospects for the food
merchant?

Despite these rising costs, I think that the prospects
are good--for the alert food merchant. Now, you notice
that I said the _alert_ merchant.

For one thing, there is a growing market. About five
billion more pounds of food were sold last year than
were consumed the year before. That is a sizable
increase.

By end of last year there were about 55 million family
units, a million more family units than the year before.
Within ten years that figure will increase to more than
75 million family units. Yes, the market definitely
is growing. More family units, more food being sold.
There is more volume ahead for the food industry. See
that you get your share of that increase in volume.

Also, there is a changing market. The eating habits
of the American public are undergoing a change.

Part of this perhaps can be attributed to the popularity of television. Many a housewife wishes to
prepare a quick meal so that she won't miss her favorite
program. Or she may serve a meal that can be carried
into the living room and eaten from a card table, in
front of the TV set. The demand for the packaged meals,
such as the TV dinner, has increased greatly.

Consider the trend toward frozen foods. They have
brought a great change in American eating habits. On
the one hand is the TV dinner, complete in itself.
But you also can select the foods for a full banquet.
As an appetizer you might serve a shrimp cocktail
using frozen shrimp. Or you might offer your guest

126

frozen melon balls. Your salad can be built around frozen Alaskan crab.

Items for the main course would almost be endless: turkey rolls, filets, steaks. And with the meat can be served all kinds of frozen vegetables, some plain, some with sauces. Various breads are also found in the store display freezers.

Desserts! What a variety! Besides ice cream, the old-time favorite but in a great many new flavors, there are pies, ready to thaw and eat or ready to bake; cheesecake and various pastries; also frozen fruits. The frozen food section of a store offers the customer a staggering number of items.

Another reason for the change in eating habits perhaps is the new emphasis on outdoor cooking. Often the man of the house is the cook for this occasion. Outdoor cooking is growing in popularity at a fast rate. This a case of combining family recreation with the meals.

Today's housewife buys about the same quantity of food that she bought five years ago, but the type of food is different. She goes in more for mixes and the frozen foods.

Mrs. Housewife of today wants more time for driving the children to school, for attending parent clubs meetings and for recreation.

The alert food merchant must adapt himself to this changing and growing market. He must attract new customers and, what's more important, hold them. The loss of a regular customer is the loss of steady revenue.

As to attracting new customers, the principal method of course is newspaper advertising. Here we might drop a suggestion. Try to make your ads appealing, as well as informative. Much newspaper advertising could be improved.

Of course, with weekly price specials in newspaper ads you can attract some new customers. But can you hold them? That is your big problem.

Holding your customers is largely a matter of merchandising and service that appeal to the customer. See that your grocery items are attractively displayed, in a logical arrangement, so that the customer can locate them easily. Keep your store lanes open, so that the customer can get to the items in question quickly. Make shopping convenient for her. Don't make her waste valuable time on needless searching.

Display of merchandise alone is not enough. In today's competitive market you need to offer a little extra in the way of service.

Last year there were 300,000 new homemakers, aged 18 years or younger. These young people know little or nothing about assembling a balanced meal. They don't know how to make a cheap cut of meat appetizing. They don't know how to make tasty sauces to go with their vegetables.

These young people and, I might add, some of the older housewives need advice, suggestions and friendly assistance while in the food store.

Here's a suggestion for you men operating supermarkets. Why not put a nutritionist on your payroll? Such an expert could be invaluable. Seasonal, changing food and meal displays could be an outstanding feature of your store. Your housewife customers would welcome the ideas she would gain from such displays. The nutritionist could also be available for personal advice on balanced meals and proper nutrition. The word would spread in the neighborhood, and such added service would both attract and hold customers for you.

The smaller merchant might say, That's all very nice, but what about us? We can't afford to hire a nutritionist to conduct such an activity.

No, perhaps you couldn't. Probably a full-scale nutrition department is out of the question. But I am sure that you could offer some service in this line. You may have at this moment a woman clerk who could perform capably in this service on an informal, part-time basis.

You men who operate small markets are aware of the informal, personal atmosphere of your establishments. A woman clerk with a definite knack for cooking could be on the lookout for the bride of 18, or the hesitant older housewife who seems undecided as to her purchases. Your alert employe can strike up a friendly conversation in which a food or meal suggestion is dropped here and there. She can do this, that is, if you free her of some of her routine duties of price-marking products or arranging stock. Your investment of some of her time each day will pay off handsomely in service to your customers.

Yes, I agree that the increasing costs connected with operating a retail establishment pose a serious

problem. Some merchants may find the problem too
great and finally will close their doors. But not
the alert merchant who sees the challenge of tomorrow--
and accepts it for the opportunity it really affords.

You are a reporter for the Star. It's a Wednesday
morning in February and city editor tells you to cover
speech at Fulton Hotel this noon. It's a luncheon
meeting of Downtown Merchants Association. You are to
cover meeting and write story for today's Star.

You check morgue and get several clippings on association.
One clipping tells you that association was organized
recently. Officers are Ralph E. Cooke, president;
John C. Princeton, vice president; Norman H. Tucker,
secretary-treasurer. Membership total, 125.

Another clipping announces that association has hired
Orson T. Smith of New York City, a planning consultant,
to make preliminary study in Jonesville and make
recommendations on reviving business in downtown section.
After association hears this report, they will decide
whether to have Smith set up program and carry it out
as consultant. Smith has been in the city several
days, and he will be speaker at meeting today. Speech
will be his report on recommendations of what could be
done.

You go to Fulton Hotel this noon to luncheon meeting.
About 100 members present. Cooke presides. After meal,
Cooke presents Smith.

The text of Smith's speech follows:

    I know you men and women are busy and need to get
back to your places of business as soon as possible,
so I'm not going to spend any time with an introduction
featuring a couple of jokes--you probably would have
heard them before anyway. I'm going to get right to
the core of the meeting--why you're here.
    You're concerned because the downtown section of
Jonesville is slowly dying commercially. You're
wondering what to do about it. Yours is not a unique
problem. Many other cities are facing the same situation.

131

You find that you're losing business to suburban shopping centers, and you wonder what to do. You have large investments in this section of the city and you want to keep on operating here.

The downtown sections of cities were ideal for shoppers some years ago. First the street cars, then buses, brought the shoppers to an area where the stores were concentrated. Stores were built in a tight area so the shopper did not need to walk far from place to place. All well and good until the automobile began to be used more and more in shopping. But downtown the stores took up all the room, so there was not enough space for parking. So shopping centers with ample parking sprang up in suburban locations.

At the same time, many people who lived within walking distance of downtown stores began to feel cramped. The buildings were getting older and older. The people had cars; they depended upon buses less and less. The hold of the central section weakened, and they began to move to the suburbs.

Consequently, the downtown stores were losing customers who were driving to the suburbs to shop. They were also losing customers who were moving to the suburbs.

Conditions became more and more severe for central sections of cities. Many of the stores either found it necessary to close their doors forever, or they moved to a suburban shopping center. More and more vacant stores in the downtown section of cities resulted. Commercial properties have become run down.

Housing in central sections of cities has become delapidated. All in all, the central section of many a city is not a pleasant sight.

Now, you're saying, What can we do? I will make some general observations upon which a specific program for Jonesville could be built.

You need to provide benefits for the potential customer, make him aware of those benefits and make him act on that awareness. That is, see that he does a good share of his shopping downtown.

For one thing, offer only good, legitimate deals to the customer. Be sure it's good merchandise. Police yourselves. Set up a membership program based on a code of ethics that will protect the buyer.

Another thing, cooperate in special bargain days as

132

to hours, gift drawings and so on. During those special
days be doubly sure of the quality of merchandise
offered.

Another thing is to encourage the development of
more off-street parking facilities. Also, make
arrangements for parking permits or coupons, and
finance their use so that customers may park at no
cost. Remember--they can park at no charge at the
shopping centers. This must be a cooperative project--
a part of your program as a group to give the shopper
some real benefits.

Make the shopper aware of those benefits by using
cooperative advertising regularly, emphasizing the
advantages of trading with the Downtown Merchants
Association members. Not spasmodic advertising,
but daily lineage in the newspapers.

The suggestions I've made would help attract the
customer who is driving to shopping centers for most
of his shopping.

Now, what about those persons moving to the suburbs.
Your city needs some urban renewal as to housing. And
you merchants should be vitally interested in such a
program. You stand to gain.

In the central area of Jonesville there are a number
of run-down houses and apartment buildings that should
be replaced. Also, there are a number of vacant and
dilapidated commercial properties that would make good
sites for multi-floor, high-quality apartment buildings.

Some of you as individuals could finance parts of such
a program. Others of you could form corporations to
carry through this work. You can't wait. You'll have
to push it and work fast.

It could be of double benefit to you merchants. The
housing properties could be a good income-producer.
Also, you would be bringing more residents back to the
central section of the city. They would be customers
for your stores.

You'll see that the suggestions I've made call for
joint effort on your part. You must look toward benefit
for the group, not just as individuals pulling in many
directions.

If you members of this association set yourselves to
the task, I'm sure you can revive downtown Jonesville.
It's been done in other cities; it can be done here in
Jonesville. If you decide to retain me and my organization, I will be glad to lend a hand.

133

After Smith's talk Cooke says another meeting of assn.
will be held next Wednesday noon. The officers acting
as an executive committee will have met previously with
Smith about program for Jonesville. Committee will make
its recommendation at next Wednesday's meeting as to
whether or not Smith should be engaged. Association
will vote on matter.

You are a reporter for the Sun, and your beat includes
schools. Central Parent-Teacher Association is having
meeting tonight at Central High School auditorium.
Speaker is Dr. Frank T. Martin of Grossboro, state
superintendent of public instruction; will speak on
school problems. Members of Jonesville Board of
Education are special guests.

Dr. Martin is native of Byron. Received A.B., M.A. and
Ph.D. degrees at Dexter. Was member of faculty, school
of education, Grossboro College, 14 years. Has been
state superintendent of public instruction for six months.
You attend meeting to get story for tomorrow morning's
Sun. Mrs. Alvin O. Lindsay, president of Central
Parent-Teacher Association presides; introduces Martin.
Following is text of Martin's talk:

Good evening, ladies and gentlemen, and thank you
for those kind words, Mrs. Lindsay. Perhaps I should
have said, Good evening, friends, for I see a number
of acquaintances whom I knew during my days at Dexter.
And I might add that those were happy days. And as I
look back now, they seem to have been relatively
trouble-free days. Even more carefree were the days
before that, in the grades and high school.
But perhaps that's typical. When you and I were in
school, there didn't seem to be so many problems as we
have today. It appeared to be mostly a case of normal
enrollments, instructional loads and physical facilities,
and satisfactory curricula and student-teacher relationships.
But things have become more complicated.
The schools have become crowded, necessitating a
continuing construction program. New buildings must
be erected and additions constructed. School districts
are finding this an ever-increasing problem.
In the past few years I have conferred with many
local school boards in reference to their buildings
programs, and one point stands out. Much of the

135

difficulty stems from poor coordination of work among the various contractors. In many cases prime contractors would complain that their highly-paid laborers were idle because another prime contractor or subcontractor failed to complete his work as scheduled. You should give consideration to the possible advantage of holding one contractor responsible for the entire construction, rather than dividing the responsibility among three or four different contractors, each of whom is a law unto himself.

Also, you hear arguments about the work problems arising when the general contractor is a "broker," an individual who does little, if any, of the actual construction himself. Often you find such a contractor inadequately represented on the job site. So there is poor supervision of his subcontractors, who are left to manage for themselves.

A "broker" may be awarded the contract as low bidder because his overhead is usually a small fraction of that of the general contractor who performs his own work. However, the additional problems encountered on the job, including excessive construction delays, outweigh any moderate saving to the city. Accordingly, it is recommended that there be a prohibition against contractors who fail to perform a mimimum specified percentage of the work with their own force.

The importance of the physical plant and its attendent construction program cannot be minimized, but it actually is dwarfed by the human element. Of top importance are the matters of adequately trained faculty and carefully conducted teaching programs. Buildings play a vital role in education, but there is nothing more important than teaching.

Of course, you are aware of the personnel shortage. Not enough candidates are being trained for the teaching profession. Also, an alarming number of teachers are leaving the profession for other callings, where the pay is higher.

Value your teachers. Set salary scales that will attract newcomers into the profession and that will encourage the veterans to remain. This is vital to the success of the local school systems. The pay should be high enough to induce top students to choose teaching as a career. The salary schedules should be attractive enough to combat the lure of jobs offered by industry to our experienced teachers.

136

Another factor in personnel turnover is the matter of outside employment. We must be realistic about this. Some school boards seem to feel that they hire their teachers on the basis of 168 hours a week. They frown on outside employment of any kind on the part of the teacher. Of course, the matter of outside employment can be abused; but there should be no objection to a limited amount of work for supplemental income. Some energetic individuals--often among the best of a teaching system--can perform some outside work without harming their effectivess as teachers. Some of these better teachers would not remain in teaching if they were denied the right to take on some outside employment. The profession would lose their talents forever.

If we encourage a limited amount of outside work, rather than impose a blanket prohibition, we would benefit in two ways. We would hold some teachers who otherwise would resign; and in other instances we would avoid inducing a policy of dishonesty, of "black market" outside employment. I believe that it should be up to the teacher. If he is able to perform his teaching duties satisfactorily while doing outside work, the school board or superintendent should not object.

We must draw intelligent students into teaching. We must encourage the experienced teachers to remain in the profession. New and enlarged buildings, containing the best of modern equipment, will be useless without adequate teaching staffs.

I am pleased with your large attendance at this meeting tonight. You are to be congratulated. It indicates a healthy interest in the welfare of your schools. Without a continuance of that interest, the several problems which I have discussed tonight would be insurmountable. With your continued interest and support, our schools will enjoy the growth and progress necessary to meet the increasing complexities of a dynamic society.

You are a reporter for the Sun. It's a Wednesday evening
early in October, and city editor tells you to contact
Miss Hazel Lee, superintendent of Jonesville General
Hospital, about new volunteer workers group.

Miss Lee tells you that new group has been organized.
They are high school girls, students at Central High
school. They're called Checks. Their uniforms are
white blouses and blue and white checked skirts. They
will do volunteer work at hospital starting in couple
of weeks. She says they will help out with some of the
work now being done by Stripes. Stripes are volunteer
adult women workers. They have been doing this volunteer
work at hospital for about three years--no, Miss Lee says
they were organized four years ago. Mrs. John E.
Zirkenback, 1942 Eaton, is president of Stripes.

You ask what kind of work they do. Miss Lee says
Stripes run snack and gift shop. She says they run
shop under supervision of paid manager, Mrs. William
S. Spencer, 508 S. Van Buren St. Shop is kept open 7
days a week for total of about 85 hours, so much of time
Mrs. Spencer isn't even there. You ask what else Stripes
do. Miss Lee says, deliver flowers, arrange them, water
them, etc.; operate library, run information desk, operate
shopping service for patients.

She says Checks will help out with some of this work.
Also, they will make tray favors for patients, scrapbooks
for children; they'll read to child patients when parents
are not around. You ask her if high school girls are
used this way any other place, and she says yes, other
cities have teen-age groups and they've done okay. She
says that volunteer work is very important. Without
volunteer help, some services would have to be omitted,
or hospital rates would be even higher than they are, and
they're high enough now, she says.

139

Miss Lee says there's plenty to do for both adult
women and teen-agers. She's sure girls will do okay.
Also, it may get some interested into going into
nursing. And there's shortage of nurses, Miss Lee
points out. She hopes program will guide a number
into hospital work as career.

You ask when they started to organize Checks. Miss Lee
says she suggested idea to Stripes last spring. It was
decided to wait until this fall, then keep it going
year-round, summer and all. Stripes said they would
help form group and would sponsor it. Committee of
Stripes named at that time; Mrs. Clarence H. Reid,
718 W. Tennessee, chairman.

Miss Lee says Checks were to meet this afternoon and
elect officers. They've conducted membership drive for
several weeks under Mrs. Reid's supervision. Miss Lee
says Mrs. Reid could tell you about election.

You call Mrs. Reid. She tells you officers elected:
Linda Lacy, aged 17, of 904 S. Lafayette, senior at
Central, president; Virginia Hall, 16, 503 E. Tulip
Dr., junior, vice president; Catherine Payne, 16,
628 W. Tennessee, junior, secretary-treasurer.

Mrs. Reid says most of girls have finished making their
checkered skirts. Any ready-made white blouse can be
worn with it. Miss Juanita A Edwards, Central High
school home economics teacher, supervised making skirts.

You ask Mrs. Reid when girls will start working at
hospital. She says that first there will be several
meetings for instruction, then schedule will be worked
out and girls will start Nov. 1. Regular schedule,
each girl several hours a week. You ask how many girls
in Checks organization. Mrs. Reid says there are 42
now, but others are planning to join.

Write story for tomorrow morning's Sun.

You're a reporter for the Sun, and the city editor has
an assignment for you. He tells you a Gulf States
lineman is handy craftsman and has done lot of work
around his home. Sounds like good feature story, city
editor says. He tells you to arrange interview and
take photographer with you for couple of pictures.

You call up family: James S. Smith, 517 South Washington.
You arrange to go to Smith home at 8 this evening. You
and photographer accordingly drive there.

You interview Mr. and Mrs. Smith and they show you about
house. Photographer takes couple of pictures and you
gather this information from Mr. and Mrs. Smith:

They've been married 9 years. Bought this house 8 years
ago. They have son, Ralph, 7 years old; daughter, Patricia,
5: son, Gerald, 3, daughter, Mary, 2.

Mr. and Mrs. Smith show you what Smith has built. Included
are:

Garage. Property had no garage when they bought it. Back
part of garage building is workshop which Smith also built.
Well-equipped with woodworking machinery. Concrete floor,
garage and workshop.

One bedroom with bath, added to south side of house.
House originally had 2 bedrooms and one bathroom. New
bedroom is large; the master bedroom.

Built-in cabinets in kitchen. Also washer-drier pipes
in kitchen hidden behind pegboard panels.

Brick patio at rear of house built by Smith. He also made
outdoor brick grill and large wooden picnic table and
benches. Finished patio this year. Latest major project.

141

Family room built by Smith at rear of house, attached at
northeast corner. Room is 20 by 28 feet. Opens onto
patio. Paneled in red oak, floored with vinyl. Ceiling
acoustical tile. TV and record player in family room.

In boys' bedroom Smith built bunk beds. Ralph sleeps on
top bunk, Gerald on bottom.

You ask Smith when he has time to do all this. He says,
evenings and weekends. He says he doesn't play golf,
bowl, go fishing, etc. Has no other hobbies. Smith
says Mrs. Smith helps him, especially with painting.

What next, you ask Smith. He says he wants to refinish
some more of furniture throughout house. Mrs. Smith
helps him when it comes to upholstering. They've
refinished several pieces of furniture.

Smith also says that in couple of years, he may add
another bedroom, especially if family gets any bigger.

You ask Smith how long he has been interested in this
type of work as hobby. He says since he took woodworking
course in high school.

You arrange for photographer to return tomorrow for
picture showing garage and patio.

You are a reporter for the Star. It's a Tuesday in middle
of June. It's about 9 a.m., and city editor tells you
that Leon A. O'Conner, president of Jonesville Manufacturing
Co., has just telephoned newspaper office. City editor
tells you to go to plant and interview O'Conner for story.
He wants to use story in today's Star.

You go to Jonesville Manufacturing Co. and are taken to
O'Conner's office. With him is Alvin O. Lindsay, sales
manager. Among products of company are several different
sized power lawn mowers. O'Conner tells you company is
going to produce new item. He says they are going to
build go-karts. Go-karts, or karts for short, are small
racing cars that hug the ground. Go-karting is new sport
that is becoming popular across nation, O'Conner says.

This is first that you've heard of sport, so O'Conner
goes into detail to explain. He says it is new type of
recreation, started on west coast about five years ago.
He says it's for whole family; father, mother, children;
old people and young people. You ask him where they
drive these racers. O'Conner says there are 3,700 special
tracks throughout country. Jonesville Manufacturing will
build track, called kartrack, three miles north of Jonesville
on U.S. 19. It will be half-mile long, paved with
asphalt; 20 feet wide. There will be two straightway
sections, plus several different types curves to test
maneuverability and speed of kart.

Lindsay says there will be sales and service store operated
at kartrack. Besides regular half-mile track, there will
be small oval track for beginners. Lindsay says there
are several thousand go-kart clubs in U.S. Lindsay says
his company will sponsor local go-kart club.

O'Conner says company has built pilot model of small racer
and will be producing them for sale by July 15. He says
kartrack will be finished by July 15. O'Conner says

143

company did not need to make much change in their power
lawn mower motor, for it to be used in go-kart. It's
one of the small motors, a 2½-horsepower motor. Kart
will be built of tubuler steel frame, small bucket seat.

Then he says to come and look at pilot model. O'Conner,
Lindsay and you go to one section of plant which is
adjacent to paved parking lot. There you see pilot
model. It is pushed out to parking lot. Wheels are
12 inches in diameter. Driver sits about 4 inches
off the ground. Because it has such low center of
gravity, go-kart is difficult to upset. They will
go up to 40 miles an hour.

O'Conner says go-kart will sell for about $350. He says
company feels it is more than just business proposition.
He says that go-karting provides recreation for all
family. He thinks good thing, gives family something
they all enjoy. One way of fighting juvenile delinquency.
Lindsay says even women enjoy the sport; many women are
members of clubs throughout country. It takes only a
minute to learn how to drive a go-kart.

Lindsay says there is national association of kart clubs.
Association sets out safety practices, outlaws running
on streets or sidewalks, orders that head gear be worn.
He says Jonesville Manufacturing Co. will sponsor local
club; will help organize it. Lindsay calls meeting for
next Monday night at 7:30 in company auditorium; public
meeting; all persons interested. Plans for club, rules
of go-karting will be explained. Lindsay says after
kartrack is built, weekly races will be held.

Besides sales and service at shop to be opened at kartrack,
there will also be rental karts, says Lindsay. It's very
popular in many cities throughout nation.

You go back to office and outline story briefly to city
editor. He likes idea and says it will make good feature
story. He sends photographer out to get picture of
pilot model. You write story for today's Star.

144

You're a reporter for the Sun. It's July. City editor
tells you there's a man living four miles west of Jonesville
on U.S. 28 who should make a good news story. His name
is Arnold G. Morgan. He says he has sent out gospel
messages in bottles, apparently for some years. And he
has received some responses. City editor tells you to
take camera along and get picture or two to accompany
your story.

You phone Morgan home. Mrs. Morgan says Morgan is at
work but gets home about 5 p.m. You arrange with Mrs.
Morgan for you to arrive at Morgan home at about 5:30
to interview him on this unique method of evangelism.

So you drive out to Morgan place. You tell Morgan you
understand he puts gospel messages in bottles and then
floats bottles away in rivers. Morgan says that is so.
He's been doing it 22 years, he says. You ask him how
he got started doing it. He says that from time he was
in grades he wanted to be minister. He said when he was
a junior in high school he became sick--tuberculosis.
He had to drop out of school. He was sick for about three
years. At end of three years he was able to go back to
school. But family was in debt from medical expense, so
he took job in a grocery store, instead of going back
to school. He paid off medical and hospital bills, but
never went back to school.

You ask how that led to message in bottles project.
Morgan says he was dejected about not being able to go
into ministry. He says 22 years ago in June he was
fishing in Benton River west of Salem, when bottle
floated along in river. Morgan said thought suddenly
came to him. He could send gospel messages out in
bottles; reach people many miles away. He could do his
own part-time evangelism work in that way. Morgan says
the next weekend he sent out several bottles with gospel
messages in them. And he's been doing it ever since.

145

You ask him how many he has sent out, and he says a
little over 3,400. He says he's got 625 responses,
including some from overseas. He says Benton River is
his favorite for starting messages. It flows into
Mississippi about 40 miles southwest of Salem. The
bottles go gown the Mississippi into the Gulf of Mexico.
He says he has put some bottles in the Mississippi itself.
And couple of times on vacation trips he's thrown some
into Gulf of Mexico. You ask him what kind of bottles
does he use. He says ones of clear glass. Whiskey
bottles that he gathers from the city dump and in alleys
are good bottles for purpose.

He takes you to his workshop in his garage. There he
has several dozen bottles ready for use. You take
picture of him and bottles. Also he shows you some
of responses. One is from youth in England. Another
from girl in Florida. Several are in foreign language
which he had to have translated. Language instructors
at Dexter did it for him. One letter of response was
from family in France, another a 11-year-old boy in
Portugal, another a man in Spain.

Morgan says he oftens buys religious pamphlets and
includes the them with gospel messages. He pays for
any expense, paper, religious literature, corks for
bottles. He says he enjoys doing it. He says it's
his additional way to serve the Lord. He's member of
Grace Methodist church. He has been working for 15
years for the Jonesville Manufacturing co. He's been
a foreman for 8 years. Besides wife, there are two
children, John 15, and Lydia, 12.

63 / ROBBERY TRIAL

It's the latter part of April. You are courthouse reporter
for the Sun. Besides routine matters on your beat, trial
is being held in District court. Judge Russel C. Jordan
presiding. Defendant is David T. Atkins, 24, of Morton.
Is charged with armed robbery. Employe of Jackson
Manufacturing Co.; commutes. Case is based on robbery
of Jonesville Pharmacy on night of March 5.

You have several clippings which give you background.
One Sun clipping for March 6 says that young man about
25 held up pharmacy at about 8:30 p.m. March 5. Armed
with revolver. Ralph E. Cooke, proprietor of store, and
Norman A Sanson, pharmacist, in store at time; no
customers. Man ordered Cooke to open cash register and
hand money over to him. About $600. Robber took money,
ran out of store and into alley, where car was parked;
drove away. Cooke looked out, but could not get license
number. Cooke called police; reported robbery, giving
description of robber: age, about 25; height, about 5
feet 10; weight, about 160.

Clippings of other stories appearing soon after robbery
include arrest of Atkins on suspicion. Answered description
given by Cooke; Atkins was reported spending heavily in
local tavern. Cooke identifies him as robber. Police
find .32 caliber revolver in Atkins' home. Atkins is
charged with armed robbery.

Trial opened yesterday. Selection of jury completed late
yesterday afternoon. Testimony given this morning.
Witnesses for state include Cooke and Sanson. Both
testify under examination of Prosecuting Attorney Frank
C. Dunlap that Atkins was man who robbed drug store on
night of March 5. They are cross-examined by Alfred D.
Gaines, attorney for defense. Insist they could not be
mistaken as to identity.

Detective Fred C. Huston testifies he arrested Atkins
for disorderly conduct in local tavern night of March 7.

147

He was loud, had been spending freely. Atkins had $178
in cash. Deputy William F. Dalton of sheriff's office
testifies he was issued search warrant and searched
Atkins home the night of March 7 after his arrest.
Atkins home is two miles west of Morton. Dalton said
he found .32 caliber revolver and $150 in cash hidden
in dresser drawer in bedroom.

When Atkins takes stand, he says he was home all evening
on March 5. Got home from work about 5:45. Never left.
Went to bed about 11. Atkins is questioned about money
he was carrying and money fround in his dresser. Atkins
says he had been "saving for months" to buy new car. Then
decided not to buy new car; decided to have old car over-
hauled later. Said that explained large amount of cash.

Mrs. Atkins also testifies. Says on evening of March 5
she and her husband had supper at about 6:30 o'clock.
Watched television until 10:30; both had snack and went
to bed about 11 o'clock.

Testimony is completed this afternoon, and then closing
arguments are given. Case goes to jury at 4:15 p.m.
Jury returns verdict at 5:45 p.m. Verdict is guilty.
Judge sentences Atkins to one year in state penetentiary.

It's October and you're covering the windup of a trial
in District Court for the Sun. Judge Russell C. Jordan
presiding. Defendant is Ronald F. Briggs, 32, of 812
S. Jefferson. Briggs being tried on charge of negligent
homicide in the death of Joan Merritt, 22, of Morton.
Traffic accident last March 14 at about 7 p.m. in city
at intersection of Illinois and Clay.

The afternoon session is about to open. You're checking
through some clippings taken from the morgue to brush
up on details.

Miss Merritt was driving east on Illinois. Her sister,
Mary, 19, with her. They were employed at Gulf States.
Stores were open that night, so after work they had done
some shopping and were on their way home in Morton.

A Greyhound bus was traveling west on Illinois. Briggs
driving north on Clay. Stop sign on Clay; Illinois is
the preferred street. Briggs' car hit left side of
bus. Bus and Merritt auto then met head-on. Joan Merritt
was killed instantly; broken neck. Mary Merritt seriously
injured; concussion and broken right arm. Briggs had
cut on head; 7 stitches; treated at Jonesville General
Hospital. No one on bus was injured.

In opening statement yesterday morning Prosecuting Attorney
Frank C. Dunlop told the court he would prove Briggs was
criminally negligent in that he had been drinking and was
speeding when he ran the stop sign.

Witnesses for the state testified yesterday. One was
the bus driver, Samuel T. Filmore of Salem. He testified
he saw Briggs' sedan coming at a high rate of speed on
Clay. Filmore said Briggs did not stop for stop sign and
that it was impossible for him (Filmore) to avoid the crash.
He estimated Briggs' speed at 60 mph.

149

Another witness for state: Patrolman Ralph E. Brennan
of Jonesville Police Department. He testified he was
the first police officer at the scene. He said he could
find no skid marks made by Briggs' car, indicating no
attempt to stop. Briggs' car struck bus about three
feet back of driver's seat. Brennan said he smelled
liquor on Briggs' breath and that he staggered after
getting out of car.

Another witness for state, Lester D. Craig, 714 W. Elm
Ave., said he was driving west on Illinois about half
a block behind bus. Saw car going south on Clay drive
out on Illinois without stopping; hit bus. Bus swerved
and struck oncoming Merritt car. Craig stopped and saw
Briggs get out of his car, holding a handkerchief to
head; head was bleeding.

Another state witness: Fred Parkinson, Rural Route 2,
Jonesville, bartender at Log Cabin Lounge, 2508 S. Clay.
Testified Briggs came into tavern March 14 at about 5:15,
stayed an hour or so. Parkinson said he served him
"several highballs," but he didn't keep count--"maybe
three or four."

Another state witness: Beulah E. Franklin, nurse at
General Hospital. Testified she smelled liquor on Briggs'
breath when he was brought to hospital for treatment.

Witnesses for the defense started testifying this morning.
One was Dr. Joseph N. Gardner. Testified he treated
Briggs in hospital for bruises and the cut on his head.
Testified Briggs "spoke rationally and coherently" in
view of head injury.

Briggs took stand this morning. Testified that he was·
upset March 14 because of death of a close friend the
day before. Admitted he went to tavern after he got
through work, but said he had only two drinks. Then
decided to drive to a restaurant in north part of city.
He said he was unfamiliar with route and street lights
at Clay and Illinois were confusing. Did not see stop
sign in time to stop.

Another defense witness takes stand this afternoon. Lewis
F. Gaines; lives at 528 E. Indiana, in the neighborhood
of the accident. Pharmacist at Jonesville Pharmacy, 306 S.

150

Clay. Testifies he is very familiar with Illinois-
Clay intersection. Drives there frequently. He says
that the placement of street lights makes the intersection confusing.

In closing argument prosecutor says Briggs was speeding
after drinking and that his car struck bus with great
force. He said, " A guilty verdict will do much toward
safe driving in Jonesville and Adams County."

Jury retires at 3:45 this afternoon. Deliberates 2½
hours. Returns with verdict of guilty. Verdict is
announced by jury foreman, Ray Bern of Salem. Maximum
sentence for negligent homicide is 5 years.

Judge does not set date for sentencing. Says sentencing
delayed until after disposition of motion for new trial.
Defense attorney, Albert R. Vaughan, says he will file
motion for new trial in a few days. Defense requests
defendant be released on present $10,000 bond, pending
filing of motion. Judge grants request.

151

You're a reporter for the Star. It is Tuesday, Feb. 15.
In a shooting on Wednesday, Feb. 9, James Stephens, 49,
of 620 N. Taft was killed.

News clippings from last week show that John G. Creel, 26,
of 442 W. Birch, was booked by police on murder charge.

In statement to police Creel said: Shooting accidental;
he and Stephens quarreled in Stephens home. Creel further
said: Stephens threatened him with 38-caliber revolver;
two men struggled; gun accidentally discharged.

Also in Creel's statement: Before the shooting, Creel
and wife, Wilma, quarreled; two days before the shooting.
Mrs. Creel went to home of her stepfather and mother, Mr.
and Mrs. Stephens, Creel tried to phone wife, but Mrs.
Stephens would not let him talk to Wilma. Creel went
to Stephens home. Mr. and Mrs. Stephens would not let
him see Wilma. Then the quarrel and struggle, and the
shooting.

Also, in news clipping: Coroner, Dr. Roland R. Klein,
said Stephens died of bullet wound; shot through the
heart.

Last Friday, Prosecutor Frank C. Dunlop said he would
present the case to Adams County Grand Jury Monday,
Feb. 14.

The Grand Jury considered the case yesterday, Feb. 14.
Witnesses included Mrs. Stephens, Patrolman Ralph E.
Brannon, Detective Fred C. Houston and the coroner.

Today the Grand Jury reports in District Court to
Judge Russell C. Jordan. The jury indicts Creel on a
charge of murder by bringing in a "true bill" report.

You talk to Prosecutor Dunlop and he says Creel's
trial probably will be set for the September term of
District Court. Creel will remain in County Jail.

You are reporter for the Sun. It's a Friday in May.
The Adams County Grand Jury is expected to report this
morning on a case in which a 5-year-old child died in
General Hospital Sunday night.

The Grand Jury in reporting in District Court to Judge
Jordan indicts the girl's stepmother, Mrs. Marguerite
Lee, wife of Rupert A. Lee, 638 E. Rose, on a charge of
murder by returning a "true bill." The Grand Jury had
considered the case yesterday.

News clippings of earlier in the week indicate the girl,
Linda, was brought unconscious to hospital by girl's
father Sunday afternoon. Child died at 8:15 p.m. Dr.
Roland R. Klein, coroner, said girl died of brain
hemorrhage; said there were bruises on face and head.

Mrs. Lee first told city police that child was sitting
on back of davenport watching TV; fell off and apparently
hit head on a magazine rack. After questioning Monday,
Mrs. Lee finally said she struck the child Sunday afternoon in the kitchen. Child fell; head apparently hit
base of kitchen stove. Mr. Lee was away fishing. When
he came home an hour later, girl still unconscious. He
took girl to hospital. Mrs. Lee said she had beaten
girl on other occasions because she was "always in the
way."

Mrs. Lee was booked on murder charge by city police
Monday. Prosecutor Dunlop said he would present case to
Grand Jury, which he did yesterday.

Witnesses before Grand Jury were girl's father, the
coroner and Detective Fred C. Houston.

The Grand Jury also reports on the case of a traffic
death. It declined to indict Joseph B. Lacy, 317 N.
Washington, but instead returned a "no bill" on a

155

negligent homicide charge.

A news clipping indicates that Lacy was driving in the
600 block of W. Kentucky last Saturday morning. John
Lockwood, 6, son of Mr. and Mrs. William T. Lockwood,
was struck by Lacy car; fatally injured; died Sunday
night in General Hospital; skull fracture and internal
injuries.

You talk to Prosecutor Dunlop today and he says that
Mrs. Lee's trial probably will be set for September
term of District Court. She will remain in County
Jail.

You are covering District Court trial for the Sun. This
is a Tuesday in September. Defendant is John G. Creel,
26, of 442 W. Birch. Charged with murder in slaying of
Mrs. Creel's stepfather, James Stephens, 49, of 620 N.
Taft. News clippings indicate shooting occurred Wednesday, Feb. 9, at about 9:30 p.m. at Stephens home. Family
argument; Stephens shot in chest with 38-caliber revolver.
Died almost instantly. Creel arrested an hour later at
his own home.

Creel's statement to police made that night: Claimed
shooting was accidental. Said that Stephens threatened
him with gun; Creel tried to take it from Stephens; in
the struggle the gun was discharged.

Testimony of witnesses for state is given today. Principal
witness for state was Mrs. Stephens. She testifies as
follows: Monday night, Feb. 9, her daughter, Mrs. Wilma
Creel, the defendent's wife, phoned the Stephens home.
Mrs. Creel told her mother that Creel and she had an
argument about his drinking. Mrs. Creel said that when
she threatened to leave him, Creel became enraged and
hit her on the face. She ran out of house and to home
of neighbor, Bruce W. Ferguson; she was phoning from
Ferguson home. Mr. and Mrs. Stephens drove to Fergusons'
and took her to their home.

Mrs. Stephens further testifies: Creel telephoned later on
Monday night. Mrs. Stephens answered; Creel was enraged;
swore; accused her and Mr. Stephens of interfering. Phoned
again the next night; wanted to talk to Wilma; Mrs. Stephens
said no. Creel became very angry; told Mrs. Stephens she
had better have Wilma return home. Then Wednesday night
about 9:30 she saw a car stop in front of the house. Near
a street light; saw Creel get out of car. He seemed to
be walking unsteadily. She told Mr. Stephens; he had
Mrs. Stephens and Wilma go into kitchen; said he'd get
rid of Creel. While in kitchen, Mrs. Stephens heard

Stephens and Creel arguing loudly in living room. Heard
Stephens say, "You go on back home. Wilma doesn't want
to have anything to do with you." Creel shouted, "She'd
be all right if you and her mother would let her along."
Argument continued briefly, then Creel shouted, "I'm
warning you; I'll fix you." Stephens then yelled, "You
get out of this house." Mrs. Stephens heard what seemed
to be brief struggle, then came the shot. Mrs. Stephens
and Mrs. Creel rushed into living room. Stephens on the
floor; Creel hurrying to door. After he left, Mrs.
Stephens saw revolver on floor.

Mrs. Stephens further testifies: Revolver was her
husband's; he had kept in desk drawer in living room
for protection. She said it had been kept there several
years, including the period when Creel and her daughter
spent their first month of married life at Stephens home
about year ago.

Another witness for state, Dr. Roland R. Klein, coroner,
testifies: Stephens was shot through heart; Klein removed
bullet from body.

Another state witness, Patrolman Ralph E. Brannon. Says
he arrested Creel at his home the night of shooting. Says
Creel had liquor on his breath.

Another state witness, Detective Fred C. Huston, testifies:
Tests showed that bullet was fired from Stephens' revolver.
Fingerprints of both Stephens and Creel found on gun.
Huston says Creel told police at police station that
revolver was discharged accidentally while Creel was
trying to take it away from Stephens. Creel said he then
panicked and ran.

Another state witness, Bruce W. Ferguson, testifies:
Mrs. Creel highly upset when phoned her mother. Face
red on left side where she said Creel had struck her.
Seemed to be frightened.

State rests its case. It's late afternoon; court is
recessed until tomorrow morning.

Assignment 67. You return to office and write story for
tomorrow's Sun.

158

Assignment 68. Now it's Wednesday morning. Defense
testimony is given today. One defense witness, Virgil B.
Gordon, assistant superintendent of Jackson Mfg. Co.,
testifies as follows: Creel had been employed at
Jackson Mfg. for 7 years; had good record. Company
records showed he had not missed a day of work in over
a year. No trouble with him. Gordon never smelled
liquor on his breath during working hours.

Another defense witness, Thomas G. Elliot, 624 W. Poplar
ave., testifies: Friend of Creel's since high school
days. Was in a local tavern on night of slaying. Creel
came in about 8, joined Elliot at bar. Creel appeared
quite sober. During conversation Creel told Elliot his
wife had left him two nights before. Said he was going
to Stephens house that night to see if she wouldn't come
back. Elliot said Creel had 2 or 3 beers. Left tavern
shortly after 9 p.m.

Creel also took stand this morning. Testifies: Was only
trying to get Wilma to come back home. Stephens wouldn't
let him see Wilma; ordered him out of house. Creel said
Stephens stepped over to desk and pulled out revolver.
Creel said he was afraid Stephens was going to shoot, so
he jumped at him, grabbed revolver. While they struggled,
gun went off; Stephens fell to floor. Creel "got scared"
and ran. Under cross-examination, Creel admitted he knew
gun was kept in desk drawer.

Mrs. Creel did not testify.

This afternoon after closing statement of defense
attorney, prosecutor gives closing statement. He tells
jury the evidence has clearly shown that Creel, knowing
where revolver was kept, had clever plan the night of
shooting. Says, "Creel deliberately started an argument,
pulled open the desk drawer, grabbed the weapon and shot
his victim in cold blood. It was a diabolical scheme,
using the victim's own weapon, trying to make it look
like an accident."

Judge Jordan charges jury. Says three possible verdicts:
Guilty of murder, if premeditated; guilty of manslaughter
if shooting was not premeditated, but was done in "sudden
passion or heat of blood"; or not guilty if accidental.

159

Jury retires at 3:15 p.m. At 5:15 jury brings in verdict
of guilty of manslaughter. Manslaughter in this state
carries sentence of not more than 10 years. Judge delays
sentencing, pending the filing of a motion to appeal.
You write story for Thursday's Sun.

This is a Wednesday in November. You are a Sun reporter
covering the trial of Ronald G. Johnson, aged 63, of 310
N. Washington. He was indicted for murder in the death
of Edward T. Norton, 40, Gulf States employe who lived
at Sterling Trailer Court, 2700 W. Kentucky. On Monday,
April 6, argument. Norton was shot twice; died in
General Hospital four days later, Friday, April 10.

District Judge Russell C. Jordan presiding. Prosecuting
attorney: Frank C. Dunlop. Defense attorney: Albert
R. Vaughan. Testimony for the state is being given
today.

Bernard E. Livingston, operator of trailer court, testifies
for state. He lives at trailer court. He testifies as
follows: On April 6 at about 5:30 p.m. he heard argument,
loud shouting, then two shots. He ran out of home-and-
office building and found Norton, lying on the ground,
moaning; near the trailer of Mrs. Rose Orlando. Johnson
stood nearby; had revolver in right hand. Livingston
had known Johnson as well as Norton for some time. He
asked Johnson what happened. Johnson, whose mouth bloody,
didn't answer; just shook his head, walked to his car and
drove away. By this time Lawrence R. McKenzie, who lives
at trailer court, had come out to see what had happened.
He and Livingston carried Norton into Livingston's home.
Livingston called Sheriff's Office. Deputy Dalton came
to scene. Ambulance took Norton to hospital.

McKenzie testifies for state: Says he saw Johnson get
into his car; still holding revolver in one hand. Also
says Johnson had handkerchief to his face; blood on
handkerchief; lip bleeding.

Deputy William S. Dalton testifies for state: Waited
at Livingston home until ambulance took Norton to hospital.
Livingston told him what happened. Dalton returned to
Sheriff's Office. Warrant was issued and Dalton arrested

Johnson at latter's apartment. In statement made to
Sheriff Albert C. Browne and Deputy Dalton, Johnson
claimed he shot in self-defense. Johnson said he and
Norton had quarreled several times over Mrs. Rose
Orlando, divorcee who lives at trailer court.

Another witness for the state, Raymond T. Brannon,
testifies. He's proprietor of Jonesville Sports
Center. Says Johnson bought 22-caliber revolver and
box of cartridges March 25.

Another state witness, Dr. Joseph N. Gardiner, testifies:
Norton died of peratonitis and other complications as
result of two gunshot wounds.

The final state witness, Mrs. Orlando, aged 36, testifies:
Says she didn't love Johnson; thought of him as a "father."
Says she first met him last January in a tavern and felt
sorry for him. He told her he was lonely; wife had died
two years ago. Mrs. Orlando further testifies that she
tried to discourage him after he started coming to her
trailer frequently. Norton actually was her "boy friend."
Under cross-examination she admitted having several
"dinner dates" with Johnson; also he gave her a portable
television set, clock-radio, food mixer, sweater and
"other gifts."

It is now late in the afternoon. The state rests and
court is recessed until tomorrow morning.

Assignment 69: You return to office and write story
for tomorrow morning's Sun.

Assignment 70: Now it is Thursday morning. Defense
presents testimony of one witness besides Johnson himself.

Fred Palmer, who lives in trailer next to Mrs. Orlando's,
testifies: He says that one night about a week before
the shooting, he heard big argument in front of Mrs.
Orlando's trailer. A trailer court light nearby, so he
could see Johnson and Norton clearly. Says he heard
Norton say, "If you don't stay away from Rose, I'll kill
you. And I mean it." Palmer says Johnson replied, "I'll
see her if I want to."

Johnson takes the stand, testifies: He was in love with

Mrs. Orlando and had asked her several weeks before the
shooting to marry him. He said she replied that she
would have to think it over. Johnson further testifies:
Norton had threatened him several times. Because Norton
much younger and also a larger man, Johnson was afraid
for own safety; so started carrying revolver. On day
of shooting, Johnson knocked at Mrs. Orlando's trailer
door at about 5:30 p.m. He went there after work.
Knocked several times, but no response; Mrs. Orlando
not home. As he turned to leave, he saw Norton hurrying
towards him. Johnson tried to run to his car, but Norton
caught him, swung him around; hit Johnson several times.
One blow hit Johnson on the mouth; Johnson went down.
Norton told Johnson to leave Rose alone. Johnson says
he got up and pulled revolver out of coat pocket. Norton
came towards him and Johnson fired. Norton stopped a
few seconds, then started towards him again; Johnson
fired again. Norton fell to the ground.

Defense attorney in closing argument says Johnson was
"victim of his own generosity." Says Mrs. Orlando had
led him on, accepted his gifts, at same time was dating
Norton. Defense attorney says Mrs. Orlando was really
the one to blame; led the two men on. Norton first
threatened Johnson, then attacked him and Johnson shot
in self-defense.

Prosecutor in closing argument says Johnson carried out
a "fiendish scheme." Says Johnson "baited" Norton into
attacking him, then shot him "to get rid of his competition."
Prosecutor asks how can Johnson plead self-defense when
he shot Norton not once, but twice.

Judge charges jury. Says there can be three possible
verdicts: murder if premeditated; manslaughter if
shooting was in "heat of blood," or acquittal if self-
defense.

Jury retires at 2:15 p.m. Returns at 4:45. Vernon J.
Smith, foreman of jury, reports verdict of not guilty.

Write story for tomorrow's Sun. Of course, verdict is
featured. However, adequate summary of yesterday's testimony, as well as today's, will be included to give
objective, understandable story.

163

It is October and you are a Sun reporter covering Adams
District Court. Civil trial, Trent vs. Jonesville
Manufacturing Co. and its insurer, Sterling Casualty
Co. of New York, opened two days ago. Judge Russell
C. Jordan presiding.

You have clipping of story appearing in Sun after
petition was filled with clerk of District Court.
Petition contended that Jonesville Mfg. was negligent
in not replacing an old wooden manhole cover on its
property. Petition also said that plaintiff, a lineman for Southern Bell, was permanently injuried because
of this negligence; manhold cover gave way when he
stepped on it. Clipping indicates accident occurred
a year ago last June. Plaintiff is asking damages:
$4,600 for hospital and medical expense; $8,200 for
loss of wages, and $50,000 for pain and suffering and
future loss of wages; total of $62,800.

You had checked defendant's answer, which was filed
with court clerk about 10 days after petition was filed.
Defendant in answer said manhold cover on company
property was clearly visible; that the plaintiff was
injured because of his own negligence in that he need-
lessly stepped on the manhole cover.

Selection of jury was completed yesterday, with Paul N.
Snyder as foreman. Alfred D. Gaines, attorney for plaintiff, in opening statement yesterday afternoon said he
expected to show that the defendant company, Jonesville
Mfg., was negligent in permitting the wooden manhole
cover to remain many years on the property, exposed to
weather. Said it should have been replaced, but instead
it was allowed to remain as a "trap." Gaines said the
result was that plaintiff was permanently crippled.
Defendant's attorney, Clinton V. Lacey, in his opening
statement blamed the plaintiff's own negligence for the
injury.

Yesterday afternoon one of plaintiff's witnesses, Howard
S. Reynolds, testified. Reynolds, lineman for Southern
Bell, who was working with Trent when accident occurred,
testified as follows: Trent and Reynolds were walking
across Jonesville Mfg. property, getting ready to repair
some telephone lines damaged by a storm of several days
before; both were carrying some equipment. Trent stepped
on manhole cover and fell into an opening for the property's
drainage system.

This morning another witness for plaintiff, Herbert T.
Eckert, city fireman, testifies as follows: He helped
remove Trent from the hole, which was about 8 feet deep.
Says grass around the manhole "nearly a foot high."
Boards of manhole cover appeared to be rotten; cover must
have been there many years.

Trent takes the stand; he's in a wheel chair. Testifies
as follows: Didn't see the manhole cover while crossing
the property. Suddenly he was down in the hole; conscious
but couldn't move. Remembers being taken out of hole and
to Jonesville General Hospital. Was in hospital two
months; then was released to go home, but has not been
able to walk; paralyzed from waist down. Has been unable
to work. Hospital and medical expenses, $4,600.

Dr. Joseph H. Gardner, final witness for plaintiff,
testifies: A vertebra was crushed. Plaintiff's condition
has improved, but doctor says it's highly probable he
will be permanently disabled; certainly can never work
again as a lineman.

Witnesses for defendants, Jonesville Mfg. and its insurer,
Sterling Casualty, testify. First one is Thomas E. Bennett,
superintendent, Jonesville Mfg. Says he was notified a
half-hour after the accident. Went to the scene at once.
Says grass was only three or four inches high; in fact,
no higher than manhole cover, since cover was resting on
a concrete rim about 4 inches high. Bennett says grass
is kept short, cut regularly.

Alfred T. Kelly, Jonesville Mfg. maintenance man, testifies: Says he cuts grass "every week or two." Says the
day of the accident he noticed the grass was "just about
even with the cement rim."

166

The last witness for defendants, Dr. Vincent T. Gray
of Ottawa. Examined the plaintiff at the request of
Jonesville Mfg. Dr. Gray says he believes Trent may
recover nearly full use of legs; should be able to work
again, though perhaps not as a lineman.

After the closing arguments of the two attorneys, the
judge charges the jury. Judge says jury must decide
whether negligence on the part of the defendant company was the sole cause of the injury or whether
contributory negligence of the plaintiff was involved.
Also, if the defendant company's negligence was the
sole cause of the injury, the jury must establish the
amount of damages.

The jury retires at 4:15 p.m. At 6 p.m. jury returns
a verdict for the plaintiff--general damages of $25,000
and compensitory damages of $12,800, covering hospital
and medical expenses and loss of wages, or a total of
$37,800. Write the story for tomorrow morning's Sun.

It is a morning in April. You are covering a civil suit
in Adams District Court for the Star. Jury trial, Judge
Russell C. Jordan presiding. Suit is based on auto
accident which occurred two years ago this month.

The plaintiff is Vernon S. Caldwell, electrician employed
by Robertson Electric Co. Suing William S. Iverson,
office manager of Wilson Foundry Inc., and his insurer,
Guardian Casualty Co. of New York. Asking $55,300.
Broken down into $3,100, hospital and medical expenses;
$2,200, loss of wages; $50,000, pain and suffering and
future loss of wages. William H. Preston, attorney for
plaintiff; Albert R. Vaughn, attorney for defendant.
Opening statements yesterday morning.

Defendant's attorney in opening statement contends plaintiff's contributory negligence was a proximate cause of
his injuries.

Plaintiff's attorney in his opening statement says he
will show that gross negligence of defendant was sole
cause of plaintiff's injury. Yesterday, late morning
and afternoon, testimony given by witnesses for plaintiff.

One witness for plaintiff, Patrolman John S. Lowery of
Police Department. Under direct examination, Lowery·
answers questions of plaintiff's attorney, Preston. Lowery
says he was called to scene of accident at Lafayette and
Tennessee at about 1 p.m. Plaintiff Caldwell traveling
south on Lafayette, Defendant Iverson going west on
Tennessee. Lowery further testifies: Left front door
of Caldwell's car was caved in about six inches where
it was struck by Iverson's car. Door glass cracked.
Preston asks Lowery how that probably was broken. Defense
attorney objects; judge overrules his objection. Lowery
then answers question: When Caldwell car was hit from
the side, apparently the left side of Caldwell's head

169

stuck door glass. Lowery says Caldwell was unconscious; taken in police ambulance to Jonesville General Hospital.

Caldwell takes the stand. Says he was driving "about 25 or 30 miles an hour when he approached Tennessee st. intersection; saw car on Tennessee coming towards him. Supposed it would stop; but driver "didn't even pause." Caldwell had no chance to avoid accident, he says. Last thing he remembers is the car about to strike door on his side. Says he was in hospital three months; unable to work at all for another 4 months. Has not fully recovered. Left knee is stiff, painful. Still has severe headaches frequently. Often unable to work a full day. Has even had to lay off work completely about one day a week.

Under cross-examination Caldwell says he doesn't remember if he had fastened his seat belt before the accident.

Dr. Joseph N. Gardner is final witness for plaintiff. Testifies: Caldwell had skull fracture on left side; fracture of left knee. Attorney Preston asks doctor if he believes a fastened seat belt would prevent a serious head injury when auto is struck from the left side. Defense attorney objects. Objection sustained.

This morning Patrolman Fred C. Denham is a witness for defense. Testifies that three months before accident he arrested Caldwell on charge of speeding on East Illinois st. Charged with driving 45 mph in a 30-mile zone. Pleaded guilty in Municipal Court; paid $25 fine.

Iverson takes stand. Testifies that on day of accident he had parked on Tennessee st. at side of Post Office (Post Office is at 400-22 Wilson, at intersection of Wilson and Tennessee.) Deposited some mail in Post Office, came back out, got into his car and started driving east toward Lafayette. He says he stopped at Lafayette, looked to the right, saw a car "about a block away," then looked to left, saw no car coming from left, so started to cross Lafayette. Suddenly saw Caldwell car in front of him. Says Caldwell must have been driving "at least 50 miles an hour."

170

Iverson further testifies: He struck his chest on
steering wheel but was not seriously hurt. He got out
and went to Caldwell car. Says Caldwell was unconscious,
lying against steering wheel. Seat belt was not fastened.

Closing statement of defendant's attorney, Vaughn. Says
it's clear that plaintiff was injured because of his own
speeding and failure to fasten seat belt. Says safety
value of a seat belt has been recognized for years, yet
plaintiff failed to take simple precaution of fastening
his.

Closing statement of plaintiff's attorney, Preston. Says
defendant is trying to say contributory negligence of
plaintiff caused the injury. Clearly proven by evidence
that plaintiff was on preferred street, defendant failed
to stop; defendant's car struck plaintiff's car at
driver's seat with such force that a seat belt would
make no difference. As to speeding, accident occurred
only 3 blocks from main intersection of downtown
Jonesville, Lafayette and Illinois. Area is heavily
patrolled by police. Very unlikely that plaintiff was
speeding under such circumstances. Preston says
defendant's negligence was sole cause of accident.

Jury retires at 10:45. You go back to office, write a
couple of other stories, stop at a nearby restaurant
for a sandwich. Then you return to courthouse. Jury
returns at 1:30 with verdict. James S. Randolph, foreman
of jury, reports verdict is for plaintiff; judgement of
$35,300. You hurry back to office to write story for
home edition.

You are a reporter for the Sun, and Dexter University is
on your beat. It's the middle of March. The Student
Government Association election was held yesterday and
you have the results for the various offices. New
officers to serve until next March. Frederick T. Guidry
of Rockdale was elected president on an anti-violence
platform. That sounds interesting, but Guidry had not
been specific during the campaign. So you decide to
interview him for a story to be run separately from the
general election story.

You locate Guidry and he gives you this information:

Guidry got idea of non-violence organization from news
story about another university. But movement there
sounded too political. Guidry says he thought idea was
too important to be hooked up with politics, whether
Democrat or Republican. He figured all serious students
should take part.

Guidry shows you a copy of by-laws of Dexter's Student
Government Association. He points to one provision that
permits the president to appoint any committee, commission
or other group that he figures he needs to help him
perform his duties. Guidry says he's going to appoint
a committee of students from both political parties, about
50-50. The purpose of the committee: enlist students
for an organization against violence on campus and else-
where in community.

If a person wants to join, he'd have to pledge that he
would try to prevent violence of any sort. That means
any activity that would disrupt classes and the orderly
operation of the university. Students are here to get
an education, Guidry points out. Attain increased
student rights? Must do it through orderly negotiation
with the administration, not violence. Vandalism?
That's juvenile. If students at 18 are old enough to
vote, they're old enough to act like adults, Guidry

says. Also, cooperation program should be carried out generally, with both university and city authorities.

Guidry says they'll devise some sort of lapel button for identification. Any kind of trouble starts--members of organization would be obligated to help settle it.

Guidry says he plans to appoint committee of about a dozen student leaders. He's already started talking with some. He wants to be sure those named will really work to get anti-violence organization going. He'll announce membership of the committee next week.

This story will carry only the new SGA president's plans for the anti-violence organization. No reference will be made to vote totals, etc., which would be carried in the general election story.

You are a reporter for the Sun. It is an evening early in February. Two local citizens come into office and confer with the city editor. They are Rev. James G. Ballard, pastor of Grace Methodist church, and Dr. Maynard D. Floyd, assistant professor of chemistry at Dexter.

The city editor brings them to your desk and tells you to get a story from them; he appears to be enthusiastic. You invite them to sit down and in your interview you receive this information:

They and a few other citizens have become alarmed by the air and water pollution of the country generally and of Jonesville and Adams County specifically. Recently about a dozen of them got together to form a temporary organization. Decided on a name: Society to Arrange for a Favorable Environment, or SAFE for short. They chose Dr. Floyd to serve as a temporary chairman and Rev. Ballard temporary secretary.

They've been making plans for an organization with membership open to the public. Group just has a temporary status now. So they want to announce an actual organizational meeting for two weeks from now on Feb. 18, 7:30 p.m., Recreation Hall of Grace Methodist church. Anyone interested in fighting pollution and in improving environment invited to attend; help form the permanent organization.

Dr. Floyd says it's vital issue for every resident of the city. Hopes group may lead to perhaps statewide organization. Also thinks organization should sponsor a symposium; have experts take part. More information should be made available to help educate the public as to the serious threat from pollution.

After the two men leave, the city editor says he believes they're on the right track. Tells you to write a good story, using all the pertinent data possible.

175

You are a reporter for the Sun. It's a Friday morning
early in May. Today the Anti-Pollution Symposium is to
be held in University Theater at Dexter. It's sponsored
by a local private group, Society to Arrange for a Favorable Environment (SAFE).

You are to cover the symposium for tomorrow's Sun. You
go to the office first and, to refresh your memory, you
look over several clippings from the newspaper library.
SAFE was organized in February of this year. Has about
250 members from throughout Jonesville and Adams County.
Officers are: president, Dr. Maynard E. Floyd, associate
professor of chemistry, Dexter; vice president, Raymond
T. Brannon, proprietor, Jonesville Sports Center;
secretary-treasurer, Rev. James G. Ballard, pastor,
Grace Methodist Church. Purpose of organization: fight
pollution and improve environment by providing more
information to the public.

You notice the program for today's symposium has three
speakers, one in morning and two in afternoon. They are:
morning, George E. Cowden of Grossboro, conservationist
for the State Department of Agriculture; afternoon, Dr.
Douglas B. Eberhart, professor of chemistry, University
of California, Los Angeles (UCLA), and Dr. Anthony L.
Bidner of Ohio State University. Bidner is a medical
doctor doing research financed by a private foundation.

You attend the sessions and take notes on the lectures.
Your notes are mostly of indirect quotation, paraphrasing
the speakers, but you have a couple of direct quotes.
Your notes follow:

Cowden: Water must be conserved; supply running short.
Just so much water. "We'll have to use it over and over
again." Some western communities have come up with good
idea: two separate water systems, a sanitary one for
drinking and cooking, the other for such things as fire

177

fighting and irrigation. As to flooding, recommends planting some land back to trees.

Eberhart: Discusses smog problem in Los Angeles Basin. Says it's come to crisis stage. Smog peaks at midday, when temperature high and humidity low in basin. Irritates the eyes. Pollution worse now than few years ago when emission controls were first put on cars. Auto exhaust serious. Over 4,000,000 cars in Los Angeles Basin. Pine trees in area seriously affected.

Bidner: Air pollution causing very serious health problems. Says small particles invisible to naked eye are worst offenders. Scientists find asbestos is a bad one. Particles of asbestos shaped like needles; penetrate the lungs. Some of sources of asbestos particles: auto brake linings and building insulation. Lead and silica are other bad lung penetrators. Auto exhaust also a big problem; carbon particles from incomplete combustion. Bidner says more research needed on easy detection of injurious, invisible particles. Industry of course causes much pollution. But burning city dumps also bad. A monitoring system must be developed to know just what the health hazard is at any given time. "Our prime concern with air pollution must be the protection of the health of the population." Bidner says people interested should push for legislation that fosters better environment, attacks pollution. People should see that they let their legislators know how they feel about it.

You return to the office and write one general story covering the symposium. When you quote a speaker, only the statements which carry quotation marks can be used as direct quotations. The rest are to be paraphrased, used as indirect quotations.

178

PART III

CITY DIRECTORY & NEWSPAPER MORGUE
OR LIBRARY

CITY DIRECTORY

The wife's name is listed with the husband, the name of the wife in parentheses: Ashley Harry J (Anna B).

Wherever possible the name of the deceased husband follows that of a widow by death: Bailey Velma R (wid Ralph E).

The place of employment and/or occupation are listed as follows: Harper Arthur M (Anna L) supt Jonesv Eng.

Unless indicated as a wife, widow or divorcee, a woman is assumed to be unmarried. The title Miss is not used in the directory.

The letter h preceding the address indicates the person is a householder. The letter r indicates he resides or rooms at that address.

Thoroughfares may be listed as avenues, drives or boulevards. Those not so designated are streets.

The name of the owner or principal official is given in parentheses after the name of a firm or institution: Jonesville Manufacturing Co (Leon A O'Conner pres)

Abbreviations

C of C	Chamber of Commerce
Colton Dept	Colton Department Store
Gafford's Dept	Gafford's Department Store
Gen Hosp	Jonesville General Hospital
Gulf States	Gulf States Utilities Co
Humble	Humble Oil & Refining Co
Ill Cent RR	Illinois Central Railroad
Jackson Mfg	Jackson Manufacturing Co
Jonesv Broad	Jonesville Broadcasting Co
Jonesv Eng	Jonesville Engineering Co
Jonesv Transp	Jonesville Transportation Co
Richardson Const	Richardson Construction Co
Sou Bell	Southern Bell Telephone & Telegraph Co
Star	Jonesville Star
Sun	Jonesville Sun
Univ	Dexter University
Wilson Fdry	Wilson Foundry Inc

181

agcy	agency	mach	machinist
assoc	associate	mech	mechanic
asst	assistant	mfg	manufacturing
atty	attorney	mgr	manager
av	avenue	optr	operator
bkpr	bookkeeper	plmbr	plumber
carp	carpenter	pres	president
cash	cashier	prin	principal
chem	chemist	prof	professor
dept	department	prop	proprietor
dr	drive	r	rooms or resides
ele	elementary	rd	road
eng	engineer	sch	school
fdry	foundry	sec	secretary
formn	foreman	steno	stenographer
furn	furniture	stud	student
h	householder	supt	superintendent
hdw	hardware	tchr	teacher
HS	high school	treas	treasurer
jan	janitor	wid	widow
lab	laborer	wldr	welder
lab asst	laboratory assistant		

A&P Food Stores (Ralph P Harrison mgr) 400 W Indiana

Abanowics Steven L (Mary) optr Wilson Fdry h 2702 Eaton

Abbott Bruce E (Catherine D) wldr Jonesv Mfg h 621 W Pine

Abney Joseph L (Martha) optr Humble h 1104 E Zinnia av

Ace Laundry (Stanley T Evans prop) 408 W Poplar av

Adams Clinton A Univ stud r 1104 W Illinois

Adams Ernest H (Wilma) mach Wilson Fdry h 1222 E Violet
   blvd

Adams Philip R (Gladys L) tchr Cent HS h 932 E Tennessee

Aikens Henry B (Julia E) prop Jonesv Cafe h 1312 W Illinois

American Legion, Butler Post 45 (John H Kline commander)
   500 W Pine

Ashley Harry J (Anna B) formn Humble h 1701 W Poplar av

Austin Anthony C salesman Decker Motor r 808 W Michigan

Austin Glenn L (Barbara S) lab Jonesv Mfg h 1012 W Tulip
   dr

Avery Sylvia B clerk Tucker Jewelry r 542 W Texas

Bacon Henry C Humble r 812 W Maple blvd

Bailey Arthur E (Rose M) city mgr h 1207 N Wilson

Bailey Norman R Princeton Furn r 709 N Lafayette

Bailey Velma R (wid Ralph E) Colton Dept h 504 E Birch

Baker Alvin C (Cora E) pres Jonesv Real Estate h 1406 N
   Clay
Baker Cora L nurse r 610 E Elm av
Baker William B (Carol M) Lockwood Lumber h 915 S Marshall
Ballard Rev James G (Martha E) pastor Grace Methodist h
   710 N Wilson
Bennett Thomas A (Margaret M) supt Jonesv Mfg h 1425 W
   Illinois
Boling Henry B (Virginia M) cash City Natl Bank h 1543
   S Clay
Borskey Ralph L (Alice B) formn Wilson Fdry h 1852 N Clay
Bossier Anthony F (Gladys E) Sou Bell h 2215 E Michigan
Boy Scouts of America, Jackson County Council (Robert C
   Lacy exec dir) 401 E Michigan
Bradford Elementary School (Phillip S Kane princ) 301-35
   W Elm av
Brannon Ralph E (Beulah A) city police h 517 N Van Buren dr
Brannon Raymond T (Mary C) prop Jonesv Sports Center h
   1233 N Clay
Briggs Ronald F plmbr Owen Plumbing r 813 S Jefferson
Briggs Russell T (Thelma S) editor Star h 1007 S Greeley
   blvd
Brooks Juanita E steno C of C r 721 E Zinnia av
Browne Albert C (Ruth L) sheriff h 900 S Taft dr
Butler Grocery (Thomas G Butler prop) 218 W Tennessee
Butler Leon G (Ruby T) optr Wilson Fdry h 1012 S Marshall
Butler Thomas G (Velma M) prop Butler Grocery h 1221 N
   Lafayette

Caine William E Jonesv Mfg r 501 W Rose av
Caldwell Anthony L (Sue) pres Caldwell Hdw & Paint h
   1541 S Clay
Caldwell Bruce R (Linda L) program director WJVL-TV h 715
   E Oak dr
Caldwell Hardware & Paint Co (Anthony L Caldwell pres)
   301-309 N Lafayette
Caldwell Vernon S (Marian E) electrician Robertson Electric
   h 125 E Tennessee
Callender George A (Linda S) Sou Bell h 821 S Marshall
Callender James R (Constance) county treas h 1235 N Clay
Carroll Herbert M (Gladys A) postman h 802 E Oak dr
Carroll Joseph W (Julia L) deputy sheriff h 717 E Maple
   blvd
Cary Henry R (Mary M) judge Municipal Court h 1602 S Taft
   dr
Central High School (Paul T Sandford prin) 401-41 N Jefferson

Chamber of Commerce (Joseph T Green sec) 307 S Wilson
Chappell Russell A (Martha M) city fireman h 322 Mason blvd
City National Bank (William E Harper pres) 100-14 S Lafayette
Civella Francis P (Constance) tchr h 2904 E rose av
Colton Department Store (Harry C Colton pres) 101-23
  S Wilson
Colton Harry C (Rose M) pres Colton Dept h 1539 S Clay
Cook Ronald B (Barbara A) lab Humble h 1220 E Violet blvd
Cooke Ralph E (Cora E) prop Jonesv Pharmacy h 1231 N Clay
Craig Katherine A prin Tanner Ele Sch h 302 Eaton
Craig Lester D (Jean M) switchman Ill Cent RR h 714
  W Elm av
Cranfield William (Linda E) mgr Martin Electric h 802
  E Poplar av
Crawford Frank S (Alta M) mgr Owen Plumbing h 617
  Adams blvd
Creel John G (Wilma V) optr Jackson Mfg h 442 W Birch
Cross Edward R Perry Funeral Home r 712 E Illinois

Dalton William F (Shirley A) dep sheriff h 304 Enterprise
Daniel Arthur C Univ stud r 1121 W Illinois
Daniels Ernest D (Linda L) city street supt h 1034
  E Illinois
Davis Mrs. Julia E clerk Gafford's Dept h 120 Mason blvd
Davis William R (Marian R) supt Young Dairy h 423 E Birch
Decker Motor Co (Norman J Decker pres) 300 W Michigan
Decker Norman J (Sarah S) pres Decker Motor h 1601 S Clay
Decker Thomas B (Kathryn) sales mgr Decker Motor h 223
  Oxford
Denham Arthur T (Alice A) Wilson Fdry h 638 N Wilson
Dennam Fred C (Ruby E) city police h 503 N Taft dr
Dexter University (James A Gardiner pres) administration
  building 710 W Indiana
Dickerson Rev Joseph R (Anna M) pastor 1st Presbyterian
  h 317 N Jackson av
Dixon Martha E sec Municipal Court r 433 Charles
Donahue Thomas E (Elsie) city streets h 705 N Wilson
Dunlop Frank C (Rose M) prosecuting atty h 1332 W Illinois

Eckard Howard L (Julia A) postmaster h 1528 N Jefferson
Eckert Herbert T city fireman r 615 S Taft dr
Eckoff Harvey R (Ruth) Jackson Mfg h 3415 W Pine
Edelman Samuel T (Martha N) Sou Bell h 3412 N Clay
Edmond Samuel F (Ellen M) mgr Gulf States h 1309 E Birch
Edwards Juanita A tchr Central HS r 733 E Illinois

Eldredge Arthur L (Barbara E) Univ dean of men h 1104
 W Texas
Elliot Thomas G (Constance) optr Jonesv Mfg h 624 W
 Poplar av
Emerson Charles E (Helen) Wilson Fdry h 220 1/2 S Lafayette
Emerson Harry B (Barbara) tchr Central HS h 1420 W Illinois
Evans Martha E (wid Harry E) steno Porter Insur Agcy
 h 732 W Texas
Evans Stanley T (Mary) prop Ace Laundry h 522 Enterprise
Evans Wesley D (Ruby M) assoc prof Univ h 604 E Oak dr

Farris Patrick N (Mary M) city engineer h 1217 W Illinois
Ferguson Bruce W (Gladys M) Jonesv Eng h 416 W Birch
Ferris Norman A (Marguerite) dep sheriff h 611 E Elm av
First Presbyterian Church (Rev Joseph R Dickerson pastor)
 301-15 N Jackson av
Fitch Fred E (Rose M) pres Jackson Mfg h 1013 N Lincoln
Floyd Maynard D (Janice E) assoc prof h 301 Charles
Foster Rev Alfred (Anna M) pastor Woodview Baptist
 h 413 W Michigan
Franklin Beulah E nurse Gen Hosp r 1133 E Oak dr
Fulton Hotel (Ernest R Payne mgr) 201-23 W Illinois

Gafford Henry C (Martha M) pres Gafford's Dept h 416
 Forest av
Gafford's Department Store (Henry C Gafford pres) 100-24
 E Indiana
Gage Paul C (Marian R) optr Jonesv Eng h 1224 E Violet
 blvd
Gaines Alfred D (Mary A) Preston & Gaines Attys h 743
 Colton
Gaines Lewis F pharmacist Jonesv Pharmacy r 528 E Indiana
Gardiner Charles (Kathryn L) sports editor Sun h 1800
 E Zinnia av
Gardiner James A (Sylvia A) pres Univ h 304 N Greeley blvd
Gardiner Julia E tchr Tanner Ele Sch r 431 W Zinnia
Gardner Dr Joseph N phys & surgeon   115 1/2 N Wilson
Gardner Dr Joseph N (Sarah E) phys & surgeon h 1319 E
 Michigan
Gilmer David T (Virginia A) dep sheriff h 507 E Tulip dr
Gilmore Mary R (wid Fred S) prop Mary's Beauty Shop
 h 331 Colton
Glaviano Peter F (Julia) Jonesv Eng h 3819 N Clay
Glowaski John B Richardson Const r 3415 W Pine
Gordon Aaron F (Barbara A) prop Gordon's Service Station
 h 413 S Jackson

185

Gordon Virgil B (Shirley) asst supt Jackson Mfg h 3201
    W Rose av
Gordon's Service Station (Aaron F Gordon prop) 200 S
    Jackson
Grace Methodist Church (Rev James G Ballard pastor) 300-12
    E Rose av
Green Joseph T (Linda L) sec C of C h 1122 S Clay
Greene Clinton R (Julia A) assoc prof Univ h 533 W Rose av
Greene Howard C (Martha E) city clerk h 412 E Violet blvd
Greyhound Lines bus station (Wesley D Martin mgr) 321-43
    W Indiana
Gulf States Utilities Co (Samuel F Edmond mgr) 1900 S Clay

Hall Albert T (Velma S) formn Jonesv Mfg h 612 N Lincoln
Hall Francis B (Ellen J) mgr Jonesv Broad h 503 E Tulip dr
Hall Glen E (Mary M) Humble h 821 Enterprise
Hall Howard A (Kathryn R) prop Jonesv Clothing Shop h
    1116 N Clay
Hamilton Guy S Parker Electric r 633 S Taft dr
Harper Arthur M (Anna L) supt Jonesv Eng h 516 N Lincoln
Harris Julia A steno Owen Plumbing r 404 N Washington
Harrison Ralph P (Cora J) mgr A&P Food Store h 700 E
    Rose av
Henderson Mrs Beulah M Jonesv Pharmacy h 605 W Oak dr
Holiday Inn (Wesley T Irwin mgr) 1800 W Illinois
Hooper Stanley T Univ stud r 413 W Rose av
Hooper Warren F (Mae L) photographer Sun h 407 Enterprise
Houston Fred C (Barbara) city police h 500 Adams blvd
Humble Oil & Refining Co (Frank R Kennedy supt) 220 S Van
    Buren dr
Hunt Thomas E (Margaret A) lab Sou Bell h 705 S Jefferson

Illinois Central Railroad (Fred Rodgers trainmaster)
    2200 E Texas
Ingram Glenn T (Martha A) Norwood Grocery h 341 Forest av
Irwin Wesley T (Mae L) mgr Holiday Inn r 1800 W Illinois
Iverson William S (Constance) office mgr Wilson Fdry
    h 404 S Washington

Jackson Alvin E (Wilma S) city police chief h 723 W Tulip
    dr
Jackson Ethel B bkpr Humble r 638 E Michigan
Jackson Howard A (Shirley A) dean Univ College of Arts
    and Sciences h 500 W Zinnia av
Jackson James V (Mary M) program director WJVL h 418
    Forest av

Jackson Manufacturing Co (Fred E Fitch pres) 2100 E Texas
Johnson Oliver B (Marguerite E) county clerk h 316 Mason
  blvd
Johnson Ronald G Humble r 310 N Washington
Johnston Bruce E (Linda L) city fireman h 505 E Maple blvd
Johnston Fred C (Marie) pres Jonesv Bldg & Trades Council
  h 1415 N Jefferson
Jones Arthur W (Jane) postal clerk h 734 W Pine
Jones Elbert F (Virginia R) instructor Univ h 614 S Van
  Buren dr
Jones Ruby S nurse Gen Hosp h 916 E Elm av
Jonesville Broadcasting Co (Wallace A Perkins pres)
  1201-19 S Jackson av
Jonesville Building & Trades Council, AFL-CIO (Fred C
  Johnston pres) Union Hall 901 N Lafayette
Jonesville Cafe (Henry B Aikens prop) 216 W Illinois
Jonesville City Hall 200-16 W Kentucky
Jonesville Clothing Shop (Howard A Hall prop) 220 S
  Lafayette
Jonesville Engineering Co (Howard E Ritchey pres) 1600
  N Lincoln
Jonesville Fire Station (William N Kennedy chief) 301-23
  S Marshall
Jonesville General Hospital (Mrs Hazel M Lee supt) 800
  E Pine
Jonesville Hotel (William R Parker mgr) 200 N Clay
Jonesville Manufacturing Co (Leon A O'Conner pres) 2300
  E Illinois
Jonesville Pharmacy (Ralph E Cooke prop) 306 S Clay
Jonesville Police Station (Alvin E Jackson chief) 220-38
  W Kentucky
Jonesville Real Estate Co (Alvin C Baker pres) 314 1/2 N
  Clay
Jonesville Sports Center (Raymond T Brannon prop) 218 S
  Wilson
Jonesville Sun and Star (Joseph W Robertson publisher)
  400 W Illinois
Jonesville Transportation Co (Frank A Prescott pres) 1700
  S Lincoln
Jordan Russell C (Marian V) Dist Ct judge h 522 W Rose av

Kane Arthur E copyreader Sun r 815 W Tulip dr
Kane Phillip S (Sarah S) prin Bradford Ele Sch h 427 Eaton
Kane Robert E (Ellen M) business rep Jonesv Bldg & Trades
  Council h 622 N Greeley blvd
Kane Virginia A (wid Norman W) h 513 W Violet blvd

Kelley Constance M dean of women Univ h 412 N Van Buren dr
Kelley Edward B (Ruth M) city police h 318 S Washington
Kelly Alfred T. (Ruby) Jonesv Mfg h 421 S Lincoln
Kelly Fred E (Anna M) supt of mails Post Office h 800 N
    Clay
Kennedy Rev Frank L (Linda E) asst pastor 1st Presbyterian
    h 312 N Van Buren dr
Kennedy Henry B (Velma A) lab Wilson Fdry h 423 N Marshall
Kennedy William N (Julia R) city fire chief h 517 Adams
    blvd
Klein Dr Roland R phys office 400 W Kentucky
Klein Dr Roland R (Elizabeth A) county coroner h 924 N
    Lincoln
Kline Aaron C (Martha E) chem Humble h 615 N Taft dr
Kline John H (Frances) prop Kline Radio & TV h 205 Mason
    blvd
Kline Radio & TV Shop (John H Kline prop) 306 N Wilson
Kline Vernon F (Sylvia J) dep sheriff h 600 E Tennessee
Kohler Rabbi Samuel B (Anna S) pastor Temple Judah h 618
    E Kentucky
Knox Lewis G (Cora M) athletic director Central HS
    h 318 Oxford
Kramer Barber Shop (Edward W Kramer prop) 311 E Kentucky
Kramer Edward W (Mary E) prop Kramer Barber Shop h 1014
    S Clay

Lacey Clinton V (Wilma C) city atty h 904 S Lafayette
Lacy Joseph B (Linda M) tchr Central HS h 317 N Washington
Lacy Robert C (Joyce E) exec dir Boy Scouts h 826 E
    Maple blvd
Lacy Warren A (Gladys A) supt Jackson Mfg h 514 W Elm av
Lampton Elementary School (Linda A Norwood prin) 700-42
    S Marshall
Lee Hazel M supt Gen Hosp h 734 E Pine
Lee Rupert A (Marguerite) mach Jonesv Mfg h 638 E Rose av
Lee William D (Rose M) sec-treas Jonesv Real Estate
    h 225 Colton
Lewis Mae R (wid Glenn T) Gafford's Dept h 1021 W Texas
Lindsay Alfred E (Alice M) mgr Sou Bell h 1214 N Taft dr
Lindsay William L (Barbara E) lab Gulf States h 613
    W Pine
Lindsey Alvin O (Juanita L) sales mgr Jonesv Mfg h 520
    Oxford
Lindsey Frank C (Martha C) Young Dairy h 506 W Pine
Litton Mack R (Martha A) prop Litton Mortuary h 404 W
    Texas

Litton Mortuary (Mack R Litton prop) 400 W Texas

Lockwood Anthony R (Rose E) mgr Lockwood Lumber h 605
  Eaton

Lockwood Fred B (Ella A) pres Lockwood Lumber h 806 N
  Lincoln

Lockwood Lumber Co (Fred B Lockwood pres) 1900 S Jackson
  av

Lockwood William T (Mary) brakeman Ill Cent RR h 511
  W Kentucky

Lowery John S city police r 416 W Rose av

Lowry William J (Gladys E) county assessor h 700 N
  Washington

MacDonald Bruce D (Mae C) mgr Robertson Electric h 204
  Charles

MacDonald Phillip F Wilson Fdry r 428 W Poplar av

Manton & West Auto Sales (William A Manton and Charles T.
  West props) 400 S Clay

Manton William A (Lula R) partner Manton & West Auto
  Sales h 413 W Violet blvd

Martin Electric Co (Howard O Martin pres) 314 N Clay

Martin Howard O (Catherine E) pres Martin Electric h
  600 W Zinnia av

Martin Raymond C Univ stud r 426 W Poplar av

Martin Rose prof Univ h 502 W Violet blvd

Martin Wesley D (Alta M) mgr Greyhound h 517 W Birch

Mary's Beauty Shop (Mrs Mary R Gilmore prop) 216 1/2 W
  Illinois

Masonic Temple (Raymond A Miller mgr) 501 W Poplar av

Mayes Dr Henry L (Kathryn A) city health officer h 631
  E Pine

McDonald Philip F dean Univ Graduate Sch h 409 N
  Washington

Merchants State Bank (James W Paige pres) 201-209 E
  Indiana

Miller Chester B (Gladys A) Humble h 334 E Zinnia av

Miller Edgar A (Marian J) partner Nelson & Miller
  Contractors h 316 Enterprise

Miller Harold T (Beulah) sales mgr Jackson Mfg h 300
  Eaton

Miller Raymond (Sylvia R) mgr Masonic Temple h 633 N
  Greeley blvd

Morris Ethel L steno Wilson Fdry r 416 E Oak dr

Murphy Rev Thomas A pastor St Joseph Catholic h 606 S
  Clay

Nash Glenn E (Kathryn M) city treas h 713 S Lincoln
Nelson Alfred T (Cora E) partner Nelson & Miller Con-
tractors h 718 E Tulip dr
Nelson Dr Edward D phys 302 Merchants Bank Bldg
Nelson Dr Edward D (Linda E) phys h 721 W Oak dr
Nelson & Miller Contractors (Alfred T Nelson and Edgar
A Miller partners) 1031 S Lafayette
Norwood Clarence S (Anna J) Jonesv Mfg h 517 W Pine
Norwood Grocery & Market (Joseph R Norwood prop) 310 E
Kentucky
Norwood Joseph R (Shirley A) prop Norwood Grocery &
Market h 631 E Tennessee
Norwood Linda A prin Lampton Ele Sch h 631 E Tennessee

O'Brien Phillip E (Margaret M) sec-treas Ruston Insurance
h 422 W Tulip dr
O'Conner Leon A (Wilma C) pres Jonesv Mfg h 1433 N
Marshall
O'Conner Lewis C plumber Owen Plumbing r 410 W Texas
O'Connor Glen B (Sylvia L) city editor Star h 923 E Elm
av
Oden Alfred A (Julia A) pres Merchants State Bank
h 1621 N Clay
O'Neill Robert P (Sarah S) dep sheriff h 614 E Rose av
Otis Martha E (wid Howard E) Gafford's Dept h 632 E Pine
Otis Russell W tchr Central HS r 638 E Michigan
Owen James M (Alice E) pres Owen Plumbing h 1100 E Illinois
Owen Plumbing Co (James M Owen pres) 312 N Clay

Parker Anthony E (Frieda E) prop Parker Electric h 722
W Pine
Parker Electric Shop (Anthony E Parker prop) 316 W Indiana
Parker Philip B (Lula J) lab asst Humble h 721 S Lafayette
Parker William R mgr Jonesv Hotel r Jonesv Hotel
Parnell Anthony L (Marguerite) pres Caldwell Hdw & Paint
h 1300 N Greeley blvd
Parnell Mack E mgr Caldwell Hdw & Paint r 1300 N Greeley
blvd
Payne Ernest R (Cora M) mgr Fulton Hotel h 628 W Tennessee
Payne Frank S (Shirley L) mgr Owen Plumbing h 323
Forest av
Pearson Clinton E (Cora A) supt Richardson Const h 713
N Jackson av
Perkins Anthony F (Anna M) lab h 336 W Elm av
Perkins Glen H (Linda L) mgr E B Reynolds h 900 E Poplar
av

Perkins Mrs. Juanita E Gulf States h 609 S Greeley blvd
Perkins Wallace A (Barbara E) pres Jonesv Broad h 728 W
    Zinnia av
Perry Frank T (Ruby L) prop Perry Funeral Home h 421
    Forest av
Perry Funeral Home (Frank T Perry prop) 500 W Indiana
Porter Insurance Agency (Leon W Porter prop) 218 1/2 W
    Illinois
Porter Leon W (Junia E) prop Porter Insurance Agcy h 405
    Colton
Portier Lester V (Rose) tchr h 3106 N Greeley blvd
Portilaski Steven S (Anna M) Star h 3108 E Illinois
Post Office (Howard L Eckard postmaster) 400-25 S Wilson
Preston & Gaines Attys (William H Preston and Alfred D
    Gaines) 310 Merchants Bank Bldg
Preston William H (Gladys C) Preston & Gaines Attys
    h 411 Colton
Price William D (Velma S) mgr Municipal Airport h 511 W
    Birch
Princeton Furniture Co (John C Princeton pres) 212-16
    S Wilson
Princeton John C (Jeam M) pres Princeton Furn h 723 W Oak
    dr

Quall Joseph E (Ruth M) tchr Central HS h 507 Charles
Quigley Robert C (Sarah) mgr Colton Dept h 1227
    N Clay
Quin Russell W (Catherine J) mgr Gafford's Dept h 904
    N Jefferson

Raborn Warren S (Kathryn) lineman Gulf States h 705 W
    Tennessee
Randall Vernon M (Elizabeth A) dean Univ College of Engi-
    neering h 633 S Van Buren dr
Randle Edgar T (Virginia S) forecaster Weather Bureau
    h 326 S Washington
Randolph James S salesman Manton & West Auto Sales
    r 520 Charles
Rarick Frank L (Cora E) business mgr Sun & Star h 306
    Adams blvd
Rarick Victoria A steno Univ r 718 S Greeley blvd
Rayborn Robert N (Shirley L) supt city schools h 400
    Mason blvd
Raybourn Mack R (Marian E) city police h 821 N Marshall
Reed Phillip H (Wilma B) lab h 332 W Birch
Reid Clarence H (Linda L) asst prof Univ h 718 W Tennessee

Reynolds E B Co dept store (Ernest B Reynolds pres)
 100-12 N Lafayette
Reynolds Ernest B pres E B Reynolds Co h 1108 N Van
 Buren dr
Reynolds Howard F (Lula) lineman Sou Bell h 415 W Elm av
Richardson Construction Co (Philip V Richardson pres)
 1400-20 E Kentucky
Richardson Philip V (Shirley A) pres Richardson Const
 h 405 Forest av
Richardson Warren A (Anna J) Jonesv Mfg h 806 E Poplar
 av
Robertson Alfred C (Margaret) pres Robertson Electric
 h 630 W Violet blvd
Robertson Clinton R (Ella L) county recorder h 413 Adams
 blvd
Robertson Electric Co (Alfred C Robertson pres) 112-16
 E Texas
Robertson Joseph W (Wilma M) publisher Star & Sun
 h 524 Forest av
Rodgers Fred (Cora L) trainmaster Ill Cent RR h 1007
 E Birch
Rodgers Samuel B tchr Central HS r 213 S Lincoln
Rogers Henry R (Marian L) chem Humble h 620 S Jackson av
Ruston Fred E (Rose M) pres Ruston Insurance h 1017 E
 Poplar av
Ruston Insurance Co (Fred E Ruston pres) 312 1/2 N Clay

Sadler Russell R (Kathryn E) carp h 604 N Jackson av
Sanders Sylvia M (wid Willard) bkpr Gulf States h 309
 Charles
Sandford Paul T (Martha A) prin Central HS h 612 W Kentucky
Sanson Norman A (Ruby L) pharmacist Jonesv Pharm h 507
 S Lincoln
Sawyer Glen B (Sarah L) adv dir Sun & Star h 914 E Pine
Scott Catherine E nurse Gen Hosp r 909 E Birch
Scott Phillip C (Arlene) director United Fund h 411
 Adams blvd
Scott Ronald F (Ellen) mgr Princeton Furn h 726 E Tulip dr
Shepard Ralph W (Linda M) dean Univ College of Agriculture
 h 412 Eaton
Smith Arthur D Univ stud r 703 W Tennessee
Smith Claude B (Shirley) eng Wilson Fdry h 911 S Jefferson
Smith James F (Linda M) lineman Gulf States h 517 S
 Washington

Smith Juanita L (wid Fred S) Gafford's Dept h 514 W
  Zinnia av
Smith Vernon J (Wilma) Richardson Const h 504 W Oak dr
Snyder Paul M (Ruth L) painter h 903 N Greeley blvd
Southern Bell Telephone & Telegraph Co (Alfred E Lindsay
  mgr) 401-19 E Indiana
Sparacello Angelo F (Marie) Gulf States h 3624 Eaton
Spence Philip T (Jane E) prof Univ h 543 W Kentucky
Spencer William R (Mary M) city police h 508 S Van Buren
  dr
Stafford Eileen L steno Jonesv Transp r 711 S Wilson
Stephens Glen D (Thelma E) tchr Central HS h 504 W Elm av
Stephens James (Ruth) conductor Ill Cent RR h 620 N Taft
  dr
Sterling Fred R Wilson Fdry r 618 N Jackson av
Stevens Marie A steno Gulf States r 513 W Indiana
St. Joseph Catholic Church (Rev Thomas A Murphy pastor)
  420-38 S Jefferson

Tanner Elementary School (Katherine A Craig prin) 520-48
  E Rose av
Taylor Leslie P (Sarah) forecaster Weather Bureau h 318
  Colton
Temple Judah (Rabbi Samuel B Kohler pastor) 600-16 E
  Kentucky
Thompson Paul A (Anna M) registrar Univ h 514 W Michigan
Thompson Richard C (Mae) Municipal Airport h 611 E Texas
Tolar Fred G (Shirley J) prof Univ h 428 W Violet blvd
Townsend Alton R (Sharon V) eng Jonesv Mfg h 315 W Birch·
Trent John E (Jane) lineman Sou Bell h 806 N Lafayette
Tucker Jewelry Co (Norman A Tucker pres) 218 W Illinois
Tucker Norman A (Julia A) pres Tucker Jewelry h 522
  Forest av

Ulmer Elizabeth R (wid Leon C) assoc prof Univ h 402
  Charles
Underwood Joseph C (Julia E) asst city mgr h 403
  Adams blvd
United Auto Workers Local 843 (Fred C Whitstone sec)
  1836 N Marshall
United Fund (Phillip C Scott director) 223 1/2 W Kentucky

Vance Anthony J (Ellen) tchr Central HS h 310 Colton
Vaughan Fred D (Alice) reporter Star h 804 E Birch
Vaughn Albert R atty 124 1/2 W Indiana
Vaughn Albert R (Margaret E) atty h 1217 N Marshall

Wall Fred B (Victoria A) eng Ill Cent RR h 605 E Tennessee
Wall Louis (Rose M) Richardson Const h 719 N Taft dr
Webb Virginia L steno E B Reynolds Co r 608 E Poplar av
Weisgerber Fred E (Julia S) Colton Dept h 3614 S Marshall
Weyerhaeuser John M (Ruby) Humble h 3816 Oxford
Wilson Foundry Inc (James B Wilson pres) 1901-31 E Michigan
Wilson James B (Ella M) pres Wilson Fdry h 1637 N Jefferson
Winston Anna L prop Winston Dress Shop h 814 E Maple blvd
Winston Dress Shop (Anna L Winston prop) 217 S Marshall
Wolfe Phillip G (Barbara R) prof Univ h 824 S Wilson
Wood Ruth E District Court steno h 621 E Poplar av
Woodview Baptist Church (Rev Alfred Foster pastor) 401-11
    W Michigan
Wright Chester H (Cora A) public relations dir Sou Bell
    h 900 W Maple blvd
Wright Paul T (Wilma S) city street dept h 703 S Jackson
    av

York Elsie M Colton Dept h 615 W Oak dr
York Joseph (Gladys L) jan Central HS h 718 N Greeley
    blvd
Young Dr Arthur F dentist 214 1/2 N Lafayette
Young Dr Arthur F (Elizabeth A) dentist h 404 Oxford
Young Bruce W (Anna M) Jackson Mfg h 211 S Jefferson
Young Dairy Inc (Louis E Young pres) 1800 N Jackson
Young Louis E (Ellen L) pres Young Dairy h 906 N Taft dr

Zimmer Anna E bkpr Humble r 407 W Violet blvd
Zimmer Fred R (Martha) jan Tanner Ele Sch h 602 E Tulip
    dr
Zirkenbach John E (Mae) formn Jonesv Eng h 1942 Eaton
Zwerdling Otto F (Catherine E) Colton Dept h 2302 W Birch

JONESVILLE STREETS

Thoroughfares in the city include the following. Those not otherwise designated are streets.

- Adams blvd
  E Birch
  W Birch
  Charles
  N Clay
  S Clay
  Colton
  Eaton
  E Elm av
  W Elm av
  Enterprise
  Forest av
  N Greeley blvd
  S Greeley blvd
  E Illinois
  W Illinois
  E Indiana
  W Indiana
  N Jackson av
  S Jackson av
  N Jefferson
  S Jefferson
  E Kentucky
  W Kentucky
  N Lafayette
  S Lafayette
  N Lincoln
  S Lincoln
  E Maple blvd
  W Maple blvd
  N Marshall

S Marshall
Mason blvd
E Michigan
W Michigan
E Oak dr
W Oak dr
Oxford
E Pine
W Pine
E Poplar av
W Poplar av
E Rose av
W Rose av
N Taft dr
S Taft dr
E Tennessee
W Tennessee
E Texas
W Texas
E Tulip dr
W Tulip dr
N Van Buren dr
S Van Buren dr
E Violet blvd
W Violet blvd
N Washington
S Washington
N Wilson
S Wilson
E Zinnia av
W Zinnia av

DOWNTOWN SECTION OF JONESVILLE

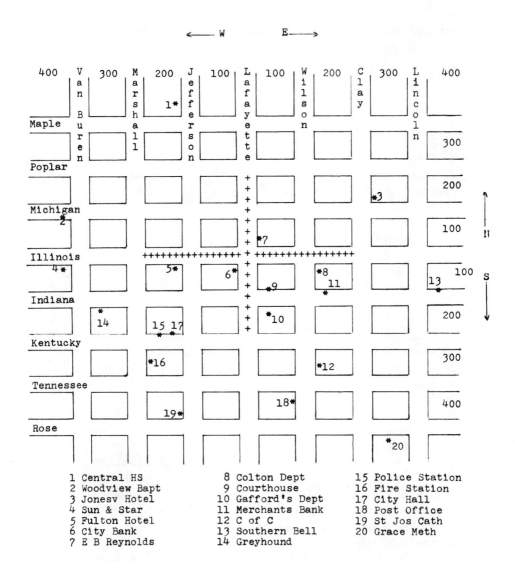

1 Central HS	8 Colton Dept	15 Police Station
2 Woodview Bapt	9 Courthouse	16 Fire Station
3 Jonesv Hotel	10 Gafford's Dept	17 City Hall
4 Sun & Star	11 Merchants Bank	18 Post Office
5 Fulton Hotel	12 C of C	19 St Jos Cath
6 City Bank	13 Southern Bell	20 Grace Meth
7 E B Reynolds	14 Greyhound	

MAP OF ADAMS COUNTY
SHOWING PRINCIPAL HIGHWAYS

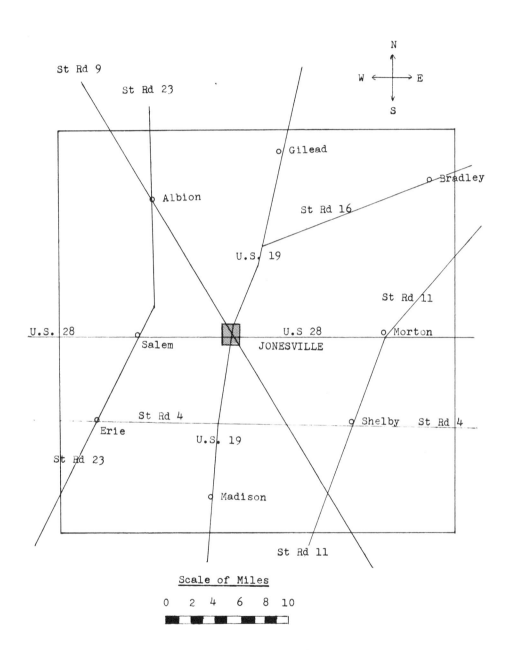

Scale of Miles

0   2   4   6   8   10

SUN AND STAR CIRCULATION AREA

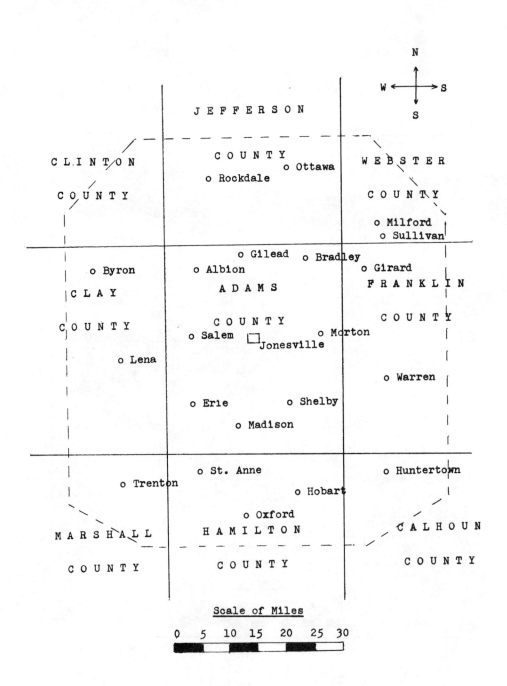

Scale of Miles

0   5   10   15   20   25   30

NEWSPAPER MORGUE OR LIBRARY

American Legion
   Butler Post No. 45, American Legion, 500 W. Pine.
   Officers: John H. Kline, commander; Anthony C. Austin,
1st vice commander; Clinton E. Pearson, 2nd vice commander;
Chester H. Wright, adjutant; Joseph L. Abney, sergeant-at-
arms; Rev. James G. Ballard, chaplain; George A. Callender,
historian; Bruce E. Abbott and Paul C. Gage, color bearers.
Bailey, Arthur E.
   City manager. Graduate of U. of Louisville, 1941.
Navy, 1941-46. Employe, Dept. of Public Works, Indianap-
olis, 1946-54. Appointed Jonesville city manager, 1954.
Baker, Alvin C.
   Mayor. Member, City Council since 1956; has been
mayor since 1964.
   Graduate, Dexter U., 1936; employe, Humble, 1936-40;
founded Jonesville Real Estate Co., 1940.
Board of Education   (see Schools)
Board of Supervisors   (see County Government)
Board of Trustees   (see Dexter University)
Boy Scouts of America
   Adams County Council, Boy Scouts of America; headquar-
ters, 401 E Michigan; Robert C. Lacy, executive director.
Phillip S. Kane, council president.
   Excerpt from a January news story reporting council
activities for the preceding year:
   Advancements earned by Scouts totaled 935 for a new
record. Of these advancements 608 were to Cub Scouts,
305 to Boy Scouts and 22 to Explorer Scouts. Seven
hundred ten merit badges also were awarded to Boy Scouts.
Bradley, City of
   Phillip T. Kline, mayor; Bruce C. Nelson, police
chief; Howard R. Lewis, fire chief.
Brannon, Raymond T.
   Proprietor, Jonesville Sports Center. Football star
at Dexter, 1948-50. Tackle on AP all-American second
team, 1950.
Browne, Albert C.
   Adams County sheriff. Graduate, Central HS, Jonesville, 1932; attended Dexter 3 years, 1938-41; Army,

1941-46; deputy sheriff, 1946-60; elected sheriff, 1960.
Building & Trades Council (see Jonesville Building &
Trades Council)
Cary, Henry R.
   Judge, Municipal Court. Graduate, Dexter, 1930; U. of
Michigan, law degree, 1933. Began law practice in Jones-
ville, 1933; elected Municipal judge, 1956; re-elected
every 4 years.
Chamber of Commerce
   307 S Wilson. Joseph T. Green, secretary.
Chappell, Russell A.
   City fireman. News story of February 1963 tells of
fire at a home on W. Kentucky. Chappell rescued 7-year
old boy; carried him through flames in living room.
Chappell severely burned on hands and face. Boy received
minor burns. Boy's name: Paul B. Lockwood, son of Mr.
and Mrs. William T. Lockwood, 511 W. Kentucky.
   Chappell joined fire dept in 1958. Graduate of Central
HS, 1958. Played on football team, 1955, '56 and '57.
Churches
                  First Presbyterian Church
   301-15 N Jackson Ave. Pastor, Rev. Joseph R. Dickerson; assistant pastor, Rev. Frank L. Kennedy, 6221 N
Clay.
                  Grace Methodist Church
   300-12 E Rose Ave. Rev. James G. Ballard
                  St. Joseph Catholic Church
   420-38 S Jefferson. Rev. Thomas A. Murphy.
                  Temple Judah
   600-18 E Kentucky. Rabbi Samuel B. Kohler.
                  Woodview Baptist Church
   401-11 W Michigan. Rev. Alfred Foster.
City Council (see City Government)
City Government
   City Hall, 200-16 W Kentucky.
                  City Council
   Members: Alvin C. Baker, mayor; Fred E. Fitch, vice
mayor; Henry B. Boling, Norman J. Decker, Arthur M. Har-
per, Ernest R. Payne, Albert T. Hall, Alfred A. Oden,
Fred E. Ruston.
                  Other City Officials
   City Manager, Arthur E. Bailey; city clerk, Howard C.
Greene; city treasurer, Glenn E. Nash; city attorney,
Clinton V. Lacey; city engineer, Patrick N. Farris;
street superintendent, Ernest D. Daniels; city health
officer, Dr. Henry L. Mayes.

City Zoning Board

Members: Alfred G. Gaines, chairman; Anthony L. Caldwell, Howard L. Eckard, Bruce D. MacDonald, Leon A. O'Conner.

Municipal Court

Judge, Henry R. Cary; secretary, Martha E. Dixon.

Police Department

Police Station, 220-38 W Kentucky. Chief, Alvin E. Jackson. Other personnel include: Detectives, Fred C. Houston, William R. Spencer; patrolmen, Ralph E. Brannon, Fred C. Dennam, Edward B. Kelley, John S. Lowery; desk sergeant, Mack R. Raybourn.

Fire Department

Fire Station, 301-23 S Marshall. Chief, William N. Kennedy. Other personnel include: Firemen, Russell A. Chappell, Herbert T. Eckert, Bruce E. Johnston.

Municipal Airport

Three miles east of Jonesville on U.S. 28. Manager, William D. Price.

City National Bank

100-14 S Lafayette. President, William E. Harper; cashier, Henry B. Boling.

City Zoning Board   (see City Government)

Colton, Harry C.

President, Colton Dept. Store. Member, County Board of Supervisors since 1958. Founded store, 1927. President of Rotary club, 1940; member, Board of Education, 1948-50.

Colton, Mrs. Rose M.

Wife of Harry C. Colton. President, Jonesville Garden club, 1946-48; graduated, Dexter U., 1923; teacher, Central HS, 1923-28; married Colton, 1928.

County Board of Supervisors   (see County Government)

County Government

Courthouse, 101-29 E Indiana.

Board of Supervisors

Members: Floyd T. Williams, Bradley, chairman; Harry C. Colton, Jonesville; Fred A. Grant, Erie; Andrew C. Smith, Rural Route 2, Salem; Owen D. Thompson, Shelby.

Other County Officials

Sheriff, Albert C. Browne; county treasurer, James R. Callender; county clerk, Oliver B. Johnson; recorder, Clinton R. Robertson; assessor, William J. Lowry; prosecuting attorney, Frank C. Dunlop; county coroner, Dr. Roland R. Klein.

Sheriff's Office

Sheriff, Albert C. Browne; deputies, William F. Dalton, David T. Gilmer, Vernon F. Kline, Robert P. O'Neill, Joseph W. Carroll, Norman A. Ferris.

Adams District Court

Judge, Russell C. Jordan; court stenographer, Ruth E. Wood.

Crawford, Frank S.

Manager, Owen Plumbing Co.; city clerk, 1952-1956.

Decker, Thomas B.

Sales manager, Decker Motor Co. Member, Board of Education since 1956; elected president, 1960.

Dexter University

Administrative offices, Harris Hall, 710 W Indiana.

Board of Trustees

Members: Alfred D. Gaines, president; Glen H. Perkins, vice president; Mrs. Alfred C. Robertson, secretary; Alvin O. Lindsey, treasurer; Rev Joseph R. Dickerson, all of Jonesville; Mrs. Harold B. Franklin, Trenton; Carleton E. Taylor, Sullivan; Frank W. Stevens, Memphis, Tenn.; Walter D. Rogers, Louisville, Ky.

Administrative Officials

President, Dr. James A. Gardiner; dean, College of Arts and Sciences, Dr. Howard A. Jackson; dean, College of Engineering, Dr. Vernon M. Randall; dean, College of Agriculture, Dr. Ralph W. Shepard; dean, Graduate School, Dr. Philip F. McDonald; dean of men, Dr. Arthur L. Eldredge; dean of women, Constance M. Kelley; registrar, Paul A. Thompson.

Faculty

Faculty members include Dr. Clinton R. Greene, assoc. prof.; Elbert F. Jones, instructor; Clarence H. Reid, asst. prof.; Dr. Philip T. Spence, prof.; Dr. Fred G. Tolar, prof.; Mrs. Elizabeth R. Ulmer, assoc. prof.; Dr. Phillip G. Wolfe, prof.

District Court   (see County Government)

Eastern Star   (see Masonic Lodge)

Erie, City of

Fred T. Thomas, mayor; Ronald E. Bowen, police chief; Ralph W. Austin, fire chief.

Exchange Club

Russell W. Quin, president; Dr. Arthur F. Young, vice president; Edward W. Kramer, secretary; Henry B. Boling, treasurer.

Fire Department   (see City Government)

First Presbyterian Church   (see Churches)

Foster, Rev. Alfred
   Pastor, Woodview Baptist church since 1955. B.A.
degree, Baylor University, 1948; B.D. degree, South-
western Baptist Theological Seminary, 1951; assistant
pastor, Northside Baptist church, Dallas, 1951-55.
Gafford, Henry C.
   President, Gafford's Department Store; member of City
Council, 1932-40; mayor, 1951-55.
Gardiner, James A.
   President, Dexter U., A.B. degree, Dexter, 1932; M.A.,
Dexter, 1933; instructor in government, Dexter, 1933-37;
asst. prof., 1937-40; graduate study, Northwestern U.,
1940-42; Army, 1942-46; Ph.D. degree, Northwestern, 1947;
associate prof., Dexter, 1947-51; promoted to professor,
1951; appointed dean, Graduate School, 1954; appointed
president, 1958. Author of a textbook on state and
local government.
Grace Methodist Church   (see Churches)
Hall, Albert T.
   Vice mayor. Foreman, Jonesville Manufacturing Co.
Graduated, Central HS, Jonesville, 1932; attended Dexter,
1932-33, 1933-34; employed by Jonesville Mfg since 1934;
promoted to foreman, 1948; Navy, 1942-46; member of City
Council since 1954; elected vice mayor, 1958.
Jackson, Alvin E.
   Police chief since 1954. Patrolman, 1935-42; Air
Force, 1942-45; patrolman, 1945-46; detective, 1946-54.
Jackson, Howard A.
   Dean, College of Arts and Sciences, Dexter, B.A. degree,
Hillsdale College, 1952; M.A. degree, U. of Michigan, 1954;
instructor, Olivet College, 1954-56; Ph.D. degree, U. of
Michigan, 1958; asst. prof. of history, Dexter, 1958-62;
associate professor, 1962-67; promoted to professor, 1967;
appointed dean, College of Arts and Sciences, 1970.
Jonesville Broadcasting Co.
   1201-19 S Jackson av. WJVL (radio) and WJVL-TV. Wal-
lace A. Perkins, president; Francis B. Hall, manager;
James V. Jackson, program director, WJVL; Bruce R. Caldwell, program director, WJVL-TV.
Jonesville Building and Trades Council
   Union Hall, 901 N Lafayette. Fred C. Johnston, president; Robert E. Kane, business representative.
Jonesville Manufacturing Co.
   2300 E Illinois. Leon A. O'Conner, president; Thomas
A. Bennett, superintendent; Alvin O. Lindsey, sales
manager.

   203

Jonesville Transportation Co.
 1700 S Lincoln. Frank A. Prescott, 4301 S Clay (out-
side city limits), president.
Jordan, Russell C.
 Judge, District Court. Graduate, Gilead HS, Gilead,
1926; attended Dexter U., 1926-29; LL.B. degree, U. of
Michigan, 1933. Practiced law, Jonesville, 1933-56;
elected district judge, 1956.
Kane, Phillip S.
 Principal, Bradford Elementary School. Graduate,
Shelby HS, Shelby, 1953; A.B. degree, Dexter, 1957;
teacher, Bradford Elementary School, 1957-64; M.A. degree,
Dexter, 1963; appointed principal, Bradford, 1964.
Kelley, Constance M.
 Dean of women, Dexter U. Graduate, Central HS, Tren-
ton, 1936; A.B. degree, Dexter, 1940; M.A. degree, Univ.
of Chicago, 1942. Instructor, sociology, Dexter, 1942-
47; assistant prof., 1947-54; promoted to associate pro-
fessor, 1954; appointed dean of women, 1958.
Kennedy, William N.
 Fire chief. Employe, Humble, 1932-34; joined fire
department, 1934; appointed fire chief, 1953.
Lee, Hazel M.
 Superintendent, Jonesville General Hospital. B.S.
degree, Youngstown college, 1935; master's degree in
nursing, Western Reserve University, 1938; nurse,
Lutheran Hospital, Fort Wayne, Ind., 1938-45; instruc-
tor in nursing, Western Reserve, 1945-53; appointed
superintendent, Jonesville General, 1953.
Masonic Orders
 Masonic Temple, 501 W Poplar av. Raymond A. Miller,
manager. Prairie Lodge No. 127, F.&A.M.; Hope Chapter
No. 79, Order of Eastern Star.
Miller, Chester B.
 U.S. Army 1942-45. City treasurer, 1950-58.
Municipal Airport   (see City Government)
Oden, Mrs. Julia A.
 Wife of Alfred A. Oden. Pianist; instructor of music,
Dexter, 1935-38.
Oxford, City of
 County seat of Hamilton County. Mayor, Harvey T.
Cook; police chief, Arthur E. Davis; fire chief, Norman
G. Hooper. County sheriff, Joseph R. Miller
Police Department   (see City Government)
Post Office
 400-22 S Wilson. Postmaster, Howard L. Eckard; superin-
tendent of mails, Fred E. Kelly.
 204

Rayborn, Robert N.
   Superintendent of city schools. Graduate, Central HS,
Jonesville, 1925; A.B. degree, Dexter, 1929; teacher,
Lena HS, 1929-38; M.A. degree, Dexter, 1936; teacher,
Central HS, Jonesville, 1938-49; principal, Central HS,
1949-55; appointed superintendent, 1955.
Richardson, Philip V.
   President, Richardson Construction Co. Graduate,
Albion HS, 1925; bachelor's degree in engineering, Dex-
ter, 1929; employe, city engineer's office, 1929-36;
established Richardson Construction Co., 1936; member
of City Council, 1946-52; mayor, 1948-50.
Rotary Club
   Alfred E. Lindsay, president; Glen H. Perkins, vice
president; Chester H. Wright, secretary; Phillip E.
O'Brien, treasurer.
Salem, City of
   Mayor, Harold C. Wright; police chief, Warren M.
Murphy; fire chief, Thomas G. Kane.
Schools
   Robert N. Rayborn, superintendent of schools, office
in Central High School building, 401-41 N Jefferson.
   Central High School, Paul T. Sandford, principal. Also
at same location, Central Junior High School, one of
three junior high schools in city. Central HS faculty
members include: Lewis G. Knox, athletic director and
football coach; Russell W. Otis, basketball coach; Samuel
B. Rodgers, baseball coach; Glen D. Stephens, music;
Juanita A. Edwards, Philip R. Adams, Harry B. Emerson.
   Elementary schools in the city include:
      Bradford Elementary School, Phillip S. Kane, principal.
      Lampton Elementary School, Linda A. Norwood, principal.
      Tanner Elementary School, Katherine A. Craig, principal.
   Excerpt from September news story: Supt of schools
reports enrollment for the city: Elementary, grades 1-6,
4,423; junior high, grades 7-9, 1,782; high school, grades
10-12, 1,177. Total, 7,382. Highest total in city's
history; also highest for each category.
                  Board of Education
   Members: Thomas B. Decker, president; Ralph E. Cooke,
secretary; Thomas G. Butler, Dr. Joseph N. Gardner,
Phillip E. O'Brien.
Sheriff's Office   (see County Government)
Southern Bell Telephone & Telegraph Co.
   401-19 E Indiana. Alfred E. Lindsay, manager; Chester
H. Wright, public relations director.
   205

Excerpt from January news story: Number of telephones
in use in city at close of preceding year, 15,643,
largest in city's history. Number added during the year,
1,218, or an increase of 8.4%.

Sterling, Fred R.
   Employe, Wilson Foundry, Inc. Member of City Council,
1952-54.

St. Joseph Catholic Church   (see Churches)

Temple Judah   (see Churches)

Tolar, Fred G.
   Professor, Dexter U. Graduate, Erie HS, 1928; B.S.
degree, Dexter, 1932; M.S. degree, Dexter, 1933; instructor, agriculture, Dexter, 1933-37; asst. professor,
1937-42; Army, 1942-46; Ph.D. degree, Louisiana State
University, 1948; associate professor, Dexter, 1948-
57; promoted to professor, 1957; author of a textbook
in animal industry.

Trenton, City of
   Phillip C. Travis, mayor; Frank L. Cain, police chief;
John B. Carey, fire chief.

United Fund
   223½ W Kentucky. Phillip C. Scott, director.
   Excerpt from September story announces opening of United
Fund campaign for funds for coming year. Campaign to end
in November. Goal is $280,000. Subsequent stories report
progress. November story gives final report; $287,435
or 102.6% of goal contributed or pledged.

Weather Bureau
   Housed in Municipal Airport building. Leslie P. Taylor
and Edgar T. Randle, forecasters.

WJVL and WJVL-TV   (see Jonesville Broadcasting Co.)

Woodview Baptist Church   (see Churches)

Zoning Board   (see City Government

REFERENCE MATERIALS TEST NO. 1

1. Give full names of the following persons:

Judge, Municipal Court_____

Principal, Lampton Elementary School_____

President, City National Bank_____

Proprietor, Jonesville Sports Center_____

City treasurer_____

2. Edit the following names. Correct any misspellings and supply any missing middle initials.

Russel A. Chappel   Phillip G. Wolf   Frank C. Dunlop

Norman H. Sanson   Joseph York   Lester Craig

3. A motorist starts at intersection of Tennessee and Van Buren and drives on Tennessee to intersection of Tennessee and Clay. He will travel how many blocks?____ In what direction?_____

4. About how many miles is it from Jonesville to Madison? Check nearest figure. 3____ 6____ 9____ 12____ 15____

5. Check cities in Sun and Star circulation area:

Hampton_____   Warren_____   Wilmette_____

Milford_____   Auburn_____   Bedford_____

Prescott_____   Salina_____   Monroe_____

Hammond_____   Fairfield_____   Salem_____

6. Who is chairman of the Adams County Board of
Supervisors?_____ The board has
how many members?_____

7. Who is pastor of Woodview Baptist Church?_____
_____. He received his B.D. degree in what
year? From what institution?_____

REFERENCE MATERIALS TEST NO. 2

1. Edit the following names. Correct any misspellings and supply any missing middle initials.

Philip E. O'Brien   Patrick N. Ferris   Charles Gardiner

Thomas H. Bennet   Fred C. Houston   William Iverson

2. Give full names of the following persons:

Principal, Tanner Elementary School_____

Chairman, City Zoning Board_____

Proprietor, Jonesville Cafe_____

Manager, Municipal Airport_____

City engineer_____

3. A motorist starts at intersection of Wilson and
Maple and drives on Wilson to intersection of Wilson
and Rose. He will travel how many blocks?_____
In what direction?_____

4. About how many miles is it from Salem to Morton?
Check nearest figure.   10____   15____   20____

25____   30____   35____

5. Check cities in Sun and Star circulation area:

Elmont_____   Camden_____   Girard_____

Montclair_____   Shelby_____   Newark_____

Trenton_____   Union_____   Utica_____

Linwood_____   Chatwood_____   Ashland_____

6. Complete full names of following City Council members:

_____Boling   _____Hall

_____Oden   _____Decker

7. Who is president of Dexter University?_____

_____ He received his Ph.D degree in

what year?_____ From what university?_____

_____

DATE DUE

GAYLORD			PRINTED IN U.S.A.